Cold War

Also by Keira Andrews

Gay Amish Romance Series
A Forbidden Rumspringa
A Clean Break
A Way Home
A Very English Christmas

Contemporary
Cold War
In Case of Emergency
Eight Nights in December
Road to the Sun
The Next Competitor
Arctic Fire
Reading the Signs
Beyond the Sea
If Only in My Dreams
Valor on the Move
Where the Lovelight Gleams
The Chimera Affair
Love Match
Synchronicity

Historical
Semper Fi
The Station
Voyageurs (free read!)

Paranormal
Kick at the Darkness
Fight the Tide
A Taste of Midnight (free read!)

Fairy Tales (with Leta Blake)
Flight
Levity
Rise

Cold War

BY KEIRA ANDREWS

Cold War
Written and published by Keira Andrews
Cover by Dar Albert

Copyright © 2020 by Keira Andrews
Third Edition. Previously published as *The Winning Edge* copyright © 2018 by
Keira Andrews
Originally published as *Cold War* © 2014 and *Holding the Edge* © 2014 by
Keira Andrews

ISBN: 978-1-988260-52-5
Print Edition

Dedication

To all the skaters from around the world who have thrilled and inspired me with their athleticism, determination, and artistry.

Acknowledgements

Huge thanks to Tatiana for her generous expertise with Russian phrases, grammar, and culture. Also to my best friend Rina for providing details about the culture of Kerala and allowing me to model Dev's family on her own. Thank you as well to Anara, Leta, and Lisa for their support as always.

PART ONE

Chapter One

December: The Grand Prix Final

DEV REACHED FOR his partner's hand, and he and Bailey glided onto the ice wearing matching bullshit smiles as a voice announced: "In second, and winners of the silver medal, representing the United States of America—Bailey Robinson and Dev Avira!"

Thunderous applause filled the arena, and flashbulbs popped as they took their bows and waved to the cheering Japanese crowd. Dev wished he could soak in their love and choke down the acid bitterness currently lodged somewhere around his sternum.

Smiles still firmly in place, he and Bailey hopped onto the carpet surrounding the podium where the gold medalists waited in all their sequined and red-feathered glory. Leave it to the Russians to make their *Firebird* costumes as literal as possible. Kisa Kostina, not a bleached-blonde hair out of place, beamed as she bent to air-kiss Bailey's cheeks.

Dev's jaw clenched as he shook Mikhail Reznikov's hand. He hated himself for the skitter of electricity when their eyes and palms met. Mikhail's lips curved briefly into an approximation of a smile. At thirty-one, with his short dark brown hair sweeping over his forehead, his steel-blue eyes, his broad shoulders and lean, tall body, and his truly spectacular ass, he was stupidly handsome.

Asshole.

Dev and Kisa exchanged air-kisses before he helped Bailey step onto the second tier of the podium. He took his place behind her and waved again to the audience while the third-place Canadians skated out to take their bows, followed by more air-kisses and handshakes. Although Dev and Bailey genuinely liked the Canadian team, this ritual was so painfully fake. They were all here to win, and there was only one satisfied team on the podium.

And satisfied the Russians certainly were. With his regal air, Mikhail was one of the most pompous, egotistical people Dev had ever met. He was the king of the pairs world, and he damn well knew it. Sharp-eyed Kisa was the ice queen, and together they were a perfect, humorless match. They kept to themselves off the ice, always civil but never friendly.

How Dev would love to see Mikhail Reznikov brought to his knees. He ignored the flare of desire in his belly at the other implications of that thought and refocused his attention on his resentment of Mikhail's place on the podium.

The Grand Prix Final was the last international competition before they all returned home for their national championships in late December and into January. Olympic teams would be determined, and then on to the Games in Annecy in February. Since he was seven, Dev had dreamed of winning Olympic gold. He was so close he could taste it.

The officials presented flowers and medals, and Dev played his jovial part. Being on the podium here meant they were among the best of the best, yet the silver medal hung around his neck like an albatross. He knew he should be grateful for what he had, and proud of everything he and Bailey had accomplished. And he was. But second place wasn't good enough.

He wanted to win.

As the all too familiar "Hymn of the Russian Federation" played, Dev watched the flags rise to the arena's rafters. Just once, he wanted the Stars and Stripes to have the middle position. Sure, he and Bailey had won plenty of competitions. They had narrowly missed making the last Olympic team, and that disappointment had fueled them. They'd dominated American pairs skating ever since. Three-time national champions. Winners of multiple Grand Prix events—including Skate America, Skate Canada, NHK Trophy, and the Cup of China.

But they'd never beaten Kostina and Reznikov. Every time they faced the Russians, they came up short. They were the reigning world silver medalists, and even though they'd worked endlessly on their artistry and connection and edges and transitions—it was never enough.

It wasn't as if the Russians weren't good. Dev could admit they were amazing, particularly on the technical side. They were three-time world champions, and when they were on, they were unbeatable. But tonight Kisa had fallen on their throw Salchow and they'd lost unison on their side-by-side combination spins. Yet they still won by eight points. *Eight!* Sure, Bailey had put a hand down on their side-by-side triple toes, but it was a minor error. It felt like the judges had decided Kostina/Reznikov were the winners before any of the pairs even stepped on the ice.

The crowd cheered as the anthem ended, and all the skaters squeezed onto the top of the podium for photographs. At five-ten, Dev wasn't the biggest of the male pairs skaters, but tiny Bailey only reached his shoulder. Mikhail stood a good three inches taller beside him, because of course he had to be better in absolutely everything. Dev grinned for the photographers and held up his silver medal as he fantasized about elbowing Mikhail off the back of the podium.

The torture continued as the teams posed for more photographs on the ice with their flags. Then it was time to circle the rink for a victory lap. Dev and Bailey stopped to hug a few fans, including Amaya and Reiko, two young women who attended almost every competition around the world. Dev had no idea how they afforded it, but he was always grateful to see them in the stands.

Reiko handed him a stuffed elephant. The elephant was the state animal of Kerala, the Southern Indian state where his parents had grown up before immigrating to the US, where Dev was born. He'd mentioned once in an interview that his good-luck charm was a tiny elephant pendant carved from jade that he wore during every competition on a silver chain, hidden beneath his costumes.

Ever since, fans had given him elephants in every imaginable form, from dolls to statues to goofy hats. He loved every single one, and his mother collected them in what she called the Elephant Room back home in Belmont in the Boston suburbs.

He kissed Reiko's cheek. "Thank you, sweetheart. Hope we'll see you in Annecy?"

She bounced. "Oh yes! We would not miss this. And we love new costumes!"

"Glad to hear it!" Dev grinned.

After NHK they'd scrapped their initial costumes, which didn't quite capture the darkly romantic tone of their *Jane Eyre* long program—officially called the free skate—set to the score from the 2011 film. Now Dev wore navy trousers and a button-down silk shirt with a simple white cravat, while Bailey's navy dress with delicate white embroidery at her wrists and around her neck perfectly set off her auburn hair, which she wore twisted into a braid wrapped around a knot. Dev had grown his thick black hair a little on top, where it curled in what he liked to think was a rakish fashion.

Reiko's smile gave way to a frown. "The results not correct. You and Bailey are true winners today. Everyone thinks this."

Amaya nodded vigorously.

"Thanks, guys. We love you!" Bailey gave them another hug before they skated on.

After yet more photos, they finally escaped backstage. Their coach, Louise Webber, walked them to the dressing rooms. Louise had been a pairs skater herself in her youth, although she'd never gone past the national level. Now in her forties, she was still in amazing shape, which she attributed to her "Asian genes." There wasn't a streak of gray in her short black hair, and while she often said Bailey and Dev would give her wrinkles when they didn't follow instructions to her satisfaction, none were in evidence.

Dev just wanted to get back to the hotel, but there was still the mandatory press conference to contend with. "Is this over yet?"

"You did your job out there. The rest of it is out of your hands. I'm proud of you." Louise gave them both a squeeze. "Don't let it get to you."

"I'm not. It's fine. I'm fine," Dev insisted.

Bailey snorted. "Uh-huh." She patted his hip before disappearing into the women's dressing room. "See you in a few."

Of the six teams that qualified to compete at the Grand Prix Final, the three who didn't make it to the podium were long gone. In the men's dressing room, the Canadian, Roger Jackman, was already zipping up his hoodie and stuffing his feet into his sneakers.

"Hey, man. I gotta call my wife back home. The baby's due any minute now and I want to catch her tonight before it's too late. Or early. I'm so fucked-up with this time change. Don't rush getting changed, okay? I need a few extra minutes. See you in the press room."

"Sure, no problem." Dev held out his fist. "Great skate tonight."

Roger bumped him back. "You too." He shrugged. "What are you gonna do, right?"

As Mikhail strode in, Roger hurried out, tapping his cell phone. Dev sat on a bench and unlaced his skates. From the corner of his eye, he watched Mikhail peel off his black bodysuit festooned with shimmers of burnt orange and red. Several feathers floated to the tile floor. Underneath he wore a black tank top and boxer briefs that clung to his narrow hips and muscular thighs.

Swallowing hard, Dev quickly stripped off his costume and transferred it to a garment bag. Wearing dark boxer briefs as well, he reached for his track pants, but found his attention drawn back to Mikhail. The arena's locker room had been gussied up with several wardrobe racks and a bank of makeup tables with mirrors and chairs. Still in his underwear, Mikhail went to one of the mirrors and leaned close.

The ego on this guy. It wasn't bad enough that Mikhail had to always win—did he have to parade around the dressing room half-naked? Still, Dev had to swallow hard as traitorous desire seared in him. Mikhail steadily met his gaze in the mirror, and Dev jerked his head away, cheeks hot. *Stupid!* The last thing he needed was to get caught lusting after this asshole.

"Don't worry, your guyliner isn't smudged," he snarked before glancing over.

In the mirror, Mikhail's brow furrowed, but he said nothing and pulled a lash from his eye.

For some reason this refusal to engage lit a fuse to the anger simmering in Dev's gut. "You know, you could lighten up once in a while. We get it, you're an *artiste*. So tortured and...Russian. With your flailing arms and your nines for Performance and Execution even though you just go through the motions. You always get nines, and I bet you did tonight, despite Kisa cleaning the ice with her ass on that throw. You guys even *fall* artistically according to the judges."

Mikhail straightened and faced Dev. His gaze raked down Dev's body and back up. Nostrils flaring, he asked, "You have a problem?" His accent was fairly thick, but his earlier years training in Connecticut gave him a strong command of English. "Talk to the judges. We don't control them."

Dev barked out a laugh and took a step closer. "We both

know your federation has the judges in its pocket. Skating has always been about politics, and no matter what scoring system they bring in—it always will be." He shook his head. "Why am I even getting into this?" he muttered, more to himself than Mikhail. He headed toward the bathroom. "Forget it."

Mikhail stood unmoving, and maybe Dev meant to get a little too close and knock his shoulder. But he definitely didn't intend to end up slammed into a locker with Mikhail gripping his arms, his eyes blazing and face twisted. Dev's skin burned where Mikhail touched him.

"You think it's so easy for us? You know nothing. Nothing!"

Dev shoved against Mikhail's chest, but he didn't budge. Fingers curling in Mikhail's tank top, Dev struggled to focus when he wanted so much to rip the cotton away and feel Mikhail's pale skin. "Cry me a river! You win everything just by showing up. You could drag Kisa around by her hair for four and a half minutes and you'd be golden."

"*Poshel na hui*," Mikhail spat.

Dev had been around Russians long enough to translate. He gritted his teeth. "Fuck you too."

Their harsh breathing filled the air, fingers digging into each other's skin, bodies so close and—

They were kissing, mouths open and teeth clashing, tongues battling as they rutted together. The metal of the locker was cold against Dev's back, but everything else was fire—desire pumping through his veins, and the unstoppable urge to get closer, closer, closer. He moaned raggedly as his brain tried to connect with his body.

What am I doing? Stop!

His body ignored him, and he spread his legs as Mikhail jammed his thigh between them. They were both already hard in their underwear, and Mikhail groaned as Dev grabbed his ass and ground their hips together. Dev hated him so much, but he couldn't stop touching. His hands roamed over the hard angles of Mikhail's body, and he panted into wet, messy kisses. Mikhail clutched Dev's hips and thrust their cocks together.

Anyone could walk in. Stop! I hate him! Wrong, wrong, wrong!

The scattered snippets of thought only made his pulse roar louder, and his balls tightened already, his body desperate for the release. They jerked together, and Dev could only give in to the madness that had taken over.

When Dev's orgasm ripped through him, his shout was muffled by Mikhail's palm slapping over his mouth. Mikhail hunched over as he rubbed against Dev in a frenzy, his quiet little gasps warm and wet against Dev's neck. He came silently, shuddering with the pulses of his release. Dev's body hummed with aftershocks, and he closed his eyes, breathing hard through his nose since Mikhail's hand still covered his mouth.

Then the heat vanished, and Dev opened his eyes. Mikhail backed up across the dressing room, shaking his head slowly, eyes wide. Dev was frozen in place against the locker, his briefs sticky, and his arms hanging at his sides. They stared at each other as the seconds ticked by.

"Gentlemen?" a man's voice called, accompanied by a sharp knock on the door. "We're ready for you in the media room."

They leaped into action, yanking on clean underwear, street clothes, and shoes in a blur of movement, not meeting each other's eyes. Dev made it out first, and he smiled and made his apologies to the officials, following them to the press room. Sweaty and sticky and in desperate need of a shower, he tugged on his fleece and felt exposed even though it wasn't as if there were wet spots on his track pants.

In the press room, the other skaters sat behind a long table on a raised dais. Kisa waited in the middle with the Canadians on her left and Bailey her right, everyone seated in their medal positions. On the rows of chairs in front of the table, the media, coaches, and various event and federation officials waited. Dev avoided looking any of them in the eye as he took his seat.

He couldn't avoid his partner, and he smiled in what he hoped was a low-key, completely normal way. His mouth felt raw. *Jesus, do I have beard burn?* Bailey's brows knitted together, and she reached up and straightened his hair. Shit. His hair.

Everyone knows! It's flashing all over me in neon letters. Neon and all caps!

Breathing deeply, he struggled to unscrew the cap from the bottle of water placed on the table in front of him. It took two tries, but he got it, and gulped. His heart pounded so loudly he was sure everyone could hear it.

"Everything okay?" Bailey murmured.

He nodded.

Under the table, she squeezed his thigh. "We're almost there. Just think—tomorrow we leave Kyoto and get to sleep in our own beds again. At least for a few weeks."

With a rush of affection, he took her hand. If there was one thing he could count on, it was having Bailey beside him. He exhaled and concentrated on her familiar warmth.

Mikhail entered the room, head high and shoulders back, his hair artfully swooped over his forehead. He managed to make warm-up pants and his red Russian team jacket look like Armani. Expression calm, he took his seat next to Kisa. While Dev wanted to crawl out of his skin with a mess of emotions from shock and anger to a shameful craving for *more*, Mikhail Reznikov appeared utterly unaffected.

Dev had never hated him more.

Chapter Two

February: The Olympic Games

"YOU NEED TO get laid."

Dev choked on his energy drink and glanced around the bus to see if any of their teammates had overheard. In the seat behind, Andrew Quinn smirked.

"She's not wrong."

"See?" Beside Dev, Bailey gave Andrew a sweet smile from her window seat. "Even the kid can tell."

Andrew squawked. "I'm eighteen! And the new men's champion! When are you going to take me seriously?" His fair cheeks reddened, the blush sweeping all the way to his blond hair.

"When you have your braces removed."

"They're supposed to be invisible," Andrew muttered.

"Besides, you don't want an old lady like me. I'd tell you to turn down your rock and roll and give you mints from my purse."

"You're not even that old," Andrew insisted. "Dev's way older."

"Dev's twenty-nine, and he's staying that way," Dev said. "Which means Bailey will be twenty-four indefinitely. You'll catch up with her soon enough, Andrew."

As the bus made a turn, the glittering expanse of Lake Annecy came into sight, an icy blue in the sunlight. The conversations on the bus petered out as they peered in awe. Nestled near the Swiss border, Annecy was often referred to as one of France's jewels. The Alps soared beyond the water, and a fresh layer of snow covered the town's narrow streets and medieval rooftops.

Bailey's green eyes glowed, and she blew out a long breath. "Wow. This is just...wow."

They'd traveled the world for competitions and seen more than their fair share of beautiful places, but Annecy had to take the prize. "I can't believe we're actually here."

"Me either." Eyes glued to the sights, she reached for his hand, finding it unerringly.

Dev squeezed her fingers. "We did it, B. If nothing else, we made it here."

"Now we just have to win. No biggie." She whispered, "Don't think I've forgotten that you need to get laid. There's a lot of hot man flesh here. Get some of that tension out."

"What about you? You're tense. We're all tense."

She flashed him a grin. "I've heard the stories about the Olympic Village. Believe me, I'll be having all kinds of sex as soon as our event's over. In the meantime I have my vibrator."

Andrew whimpered.

"But seriously, D. The past few days you've been so wired. We're all nervous, but..." She turned away from the window. "You'd tell me if something's wrong." It wasn't a question.

"Of course. I'm just wound up. It's the Olympics!"

She shuddered with excitement and bounced in her seat. "We're at the Olympics! I finally made it."

Andrew hooted, and Dev high-fived a short-track speed skater who'd begun running up and down the aisle as the bus buzzed again with laughter and chatter. It had been eight years, but Dev had made it back to the Olympics. He had the right partner, and he was trained and ready.

Now he just needed to get a certain Russian competitor out of his head.

After the Grand Prix Final, he'd written off what happened in the locker room as temporary insanity and focused all his energy on preparing for Nationals in January. He and Bailey hadn't been perfect, but they'd easily won their fourth US title. They were training hard to put the finishing touches on their programs and make them the best they could be. Aside from the usual aches and pains that went along with being professional athletes, they were injury free. Everything was in place.

So why did Dev feel as if he was balancing on a precipice? He'd competed against Mikhail Reznikov since they were juniors. Why should it be any different now?

Because we shared orgasms.

More than that, Mikhail had taken on the starring role in Dev's jerk-off fantasies. Every time he tried to watch porn and think of other men—*any* other man would do—his brain refused. The only way he could get off these days was to think of Mikhail and remember the sensation of his hard body and the taste of his mouth. God, that mouth. Dev imagined fucking it with Mikhail on his knees and then pulling out and flipping him over and taking his ass and—

Coughing, Dev shifted in his seat and crossed his legs into the aisle. Bailey was right. He needed to get laid. The opening ceremony was in a week, and their short program was two days later. Sex was the last thing he should be thinking of before the most important competition of his life, but maybe a bathroom blowjob would take the edge off.

Gabby, one of the figure skating federation's young media coordinators, appeared in the aisle with her usual wide smile, her tight dark curls bouncing around her ears. She gripped the edge of a seat as the bus made another turn.

"Hey, guys! The AP reporter wants to move up your interview. When we get to the village, I'll take you to the media center and you'll have your sit-down right away. Okay?"

"Sure, Gabby. No problem," Bailey replied.

"You got your copies of Sue's talking points, right? She wanted to make sure you stayed on message." Gabby smiled awkwardly.

Dev nodded. "Don't worry. We know the drill."

"Oh of course. She just wanted to…" Gabby seemed to be trying to find the most diplomatic phrasing.

"Make sure we show absolutely no personality and are blandly inoffensive?" Bailey suggested.

Gabby tried to laugh. "Well, she just wants to be sure American figure skating is portrayed in the best possible light."

As Bailey opened her mouth, Dev cut her off. "It's okay. We understand. Right, B?"

She smiled sweetly. "Yes. I promise we won't say anything about how we're hoping Kisa Kostina and Mikhail Reznikov will implode spectacularly and miss half their elements."

Gabby appeared extremely constipated.

With a sigh, Bailey squeezed Gabby's arm. "Seriously. Don't worry about it. We know you're just doing your job, and we'll do ours. Promise."

They both smiled at Gabby before she returned to her seat. The mention of Mikhail had Dev's mind spinning off in entirely inappropriate directions and he refocused. "You sure you're up for this?"

"It's fine. You know I give good interview. I may not always follow the talking points quite to the letter, but close enough."

He snorted. "I don't think Sue Stabler and the rest of the Feds would agree."

"They can't see the forest for the trees. Honestly, what figure skating in America needs is *personality*. When we're all pleasant little ciphers, it doesn't draw in the viewers. Remember Matty Marcus? He was the *best*. That's what we need. Personality."

"You know I'm on board, B. Look, we try our best to be ourselves while still playing the game. God, I will not miss the politics in this sport." He groaned softly. "Could I feel like being interviewed any less right now? We just got off a plane. I don't even know what time it is."

"It's"—Bailey pulled out her phone—"eight-twenty a.m., and we have to stay up all day anyway to beat the jet lag. Might as well be our charming selves for the press and get some attention. Unless you wanted to go get laid."

"You have a one-track mind."

"It's true. I'm a huge perv. But it's one of the things you love most about me."

Laughing, Dev pressed a kiss to her head. "I can't deny it."

Andrew cleared his throat behind them. "So if you're such a perv—"

"Not gonna happen."

"But—"

As Bailey and Andrew bickered, Dev closed his eyes and did some deep-breathing exercises. It would be fine. Everything was fine. When he and Mikhail saw each other again, it would be the same as always. Dev would smile and pal around with the affable Chinese skaters, and Roger Jackman would tell dirty jokes while Mikhail ignored everyone, aloof as always. Nothing had changed, and nothing would.

"DEV, YOU FIRST competed at the Olympic Games eight years ago with your former partner. How is this experience different?"

Smiling easily, Dev tried to relax. They were holed up in what was called an interview suite. In reality, it was little more than a small windowless room with three hard-backed chairs facing one another. "Well, I'm older now, and I hope wiser. The first time I wasn't a medal contender, so it was all about the experience. This time around, expectations are much higher."

The middle-aged American reporter, who'd introduced himself as Rich with a firm handshake and efficient smile, addressed Bailey. "Are you feeling the weight of those expectations? How do you cope with the pressure?"

For a split second Dev was afraid she might say her vibrator, but of course Bailey was on her best media-friendly behavior.

"I have a great support system. My family and friends are always there for me, as well as our coaches and teammates. And of course Dev is a constant source of strength. We just remind each other that no matter what happens, we're going to do our best and soak up every moment of this experience."

"Are you disappointed the team event was abolished after its trial run in Sochi?"

Dev and Bailey shared a glance, and Dev answered for them. "Yes and no. Of course it would be great to go for a medal together with our teammates in ice dance and singles, but it was a lot to ask to do our programs twice in competition, especially for the pairs since we're first up and the team event was at the beginning of the Games."

"Do you think you have a shot at the gold? The Russians dominated pairs skating for decades, and with Kostina/Reznikov they've returned to the top of the sport. Many say they're unbeatable."

Bailey's smile was razor sharp, but she kept her tone light. "You never know what's going to happen on the day. We've worked our whole lives for this, and we're going to give a hundred and ten percent. We absolutely believe we can win."

"You also face stiff competition from the Canadians and Chinese," Rich noted.

Dev jumped in. "Absolutely. Nothing's guaranteed for any team." *Except the Russians since the judges think they shit gold.* "We all have to go for it, and we'll see who comes out on top."

"There's been a great deal of controversy regarding the judging system for several years now. Do you think there's still too much room for bias in the system?"

Do one-legged ducks swim in circles? Dev kept his expression placid. "Skating will always be a subjective sport. Sometimes we don't agree with the judges' marks, but my mother used to tell me, 'trying to please everybody is like asking a goat to be an elephant.'" He chuckled. "I think it makes more sense in Malayalam. But possibly not."

Rich smiled. "Speaking of your family, I'm told you've become quite the celebrity in southern India. When was the last time you visited?"

"Not since I was a teenager, but I'd love to go back. The support has been amazing. Not just from Kerala, but from all of India and the Indian communities in the States. A lot of people have told me they'd never watched skating before, and I think it's wonderful for our sport to become more multicultural."

"How did you both get started in figure skating?"

Bailey glanced at him and spoke first. "I can remember watching the Olympics on TV when I was a little girl in Evanston. I told my parents I was going to do that someday. They just laughed and thought I'd forget about it, but for the next week I nagged them about taking skating lessons. And here I am." She grinned. "At the Olympics. I have to pinch myself sometimes. Dev wanted to be a hockey star first, but he came around."

Dev chuckled. "I sure did. My parents put me in all the sports they considered quintessentially American. Baseball, of course, and football, and hockey. There were elite figure skaters at the rink, and I loved the way they spun and jumped. I knocked out my front tooth trying a jump without a toe pick. After that, my parents bought me figure skates. I'd always loved music as a kid, and the idea of mixing music and sports was just perfect to me. Our extended family thought my parents were nuts. They said Indian boys don't skate. But they came around."

"When you and Bailey won your first US title, there was a spate of vicious, racist comments on Twitter. How did you handle that?"

Dev shrugged. "There will always be ignorant people who call me a terrorist because of the color of my skin, or who say I'm lying about my family's religion. Just like the States, India's a diverse country. Where my parents come from, twenty percent of the population is Christian. But if people want to believe I'm a secret Muslim, at least I'm in good company."

Rich chuckled. "Indeed. Bailey, how does it affect you when Dev is attacked?"

"It really makes my blood boil."

"And trust me when I say you don't want to get on Bailey's bad side. She may look delicate, but she's tough as nails," Dev added.

Bailey smiled. "Fortunately the vast majority of people out there are supportive, and we ignore the bigots. They're not worth it."

"Dev, you mentioned Bailey's tough. I'd think you'd have to be, not only as an athlete, but as a female pairs skater. The lifts and throws can be incredibly dangerous. Do you ever get scared, Bailey?" Rich asked.

"Never. I trust Dev completely, and I love to fly. It's the whole reason I became a pairs skater. Throw me, twist me, spin me—I love every second. He hasn't dropped me yet." She grinned.

Dev groaned. "Quick, everyone knock on wood." He rapped his knuckles on his own head. "I obviously know a lot of figure skaters, and pair girls are a breed apart. They're fierce. Bailey inspires me every day."

Rich scanned his notes. "You're considered by many to be the greatest American pairs team since Babilonia/Gardner. In the decade before you became champions, we saw a revolving door of teams at the top, with none able to achieve international success.

You won your fourth national title last month and regularly stand on international podiums. What's the secret to your success?"

"Obviously a lot of hard work, but I think one thing that's set us apart is that we've actually stayed together for more than five minutes," Dev answered with a smile. "You can't throw in the towel as soon as something goes wrong. When we teamed up, we committed to the long haul. It took a couple years for everything to gel. We had to be patient."

As they answered the standard questions about training and preparation, Dev found himself wishing he had a coffee. Not that he was really supposed to be drinking coffee, but it was going to be a long day without one and everyone had to have a vice, right? They had to be at the practice rink in the morning, and the thought made him want to curl up and take a nap.

"You've said you'll be retiring at the end of this season. What are your plans for life after skating?"

Dev's mother had been asking the same question for two years. Dev glanced at Bailey. "Well, we'd both love to keep skating together professionally in shows and competitions like the Japan Open. There aren't as many opportunities for professional skaters as there once were, unfortunately. I'd love to get into coaching in the future. I'm so passionate about the sport."

"Honestly, it's almost impossible to think of anything past the next two weeks. Our whole lives, and especially this past year, have been focused on the Olympics. It's like..." Bailey trailed off. "Like tunnel vision. We know there's a whole world waiting for us once we've finished competing, but it's theoretical. I'd like to go to college and travel, but right now everything comes down to these Games."

"There's often a drop-off in competitors for the world championships in March after an Olympic Games, many citing exhaustion and the difficulty in revving up for another major competition so quickly. But you've said you definitely plan on competing, especially since the event will be in Dev's hometown of Boston."

Dev smiled. "Absolutely. We're really looking forward to it." Truthfully they couldn't even deal with thinking about it until after the Olympics were in the record books. One thing at a time. "It's quite challenging after a huge event to get back to the practice rink and do it all over again in a few short weeks. But we can't pass up the chance to perform for so many friends and family. While we train in Colorado Springs, we're both from the northeast and this will be a homecoming."

"Did you consider continuing on past this season and competing for another four years? Top pair teams are usually on the older side for skaters, and it's possible you could still be contenders for a few years to come."

Bailey glanced at Dev, and then answered for them. "We did consider it very carefully, of course. But we feel like the time is right to move on and put competition behind us. We've worked so hard to be our very best, and maintaining that form for another Olympic cycle would be very difficult. We've accomplished so much, and we want to go out on a high note. On our terms."

"Well, I wish you the best of luck here in Annecy and in the future," Rich said, switching off his recorder.

After handshakes and thank-yous, Gabby appeared as if from thin air with clipboard in hand and escorted them through the teeming media center.

"All right. I don't have anything for you tomorrow, but filming for the NBC fluff piece will be the next morning. I'll meet you here at nine sharp. Do you know where the shuttle stop is? Should I walk you there?"

"We'll find it," Bailey said. "Thanks!" She tugged on Dev's arm and led him out into the sunshine and frosty air. "God, I just want a shower. I must stink."

Dev shrugged. "No more than usual."

Bailey ignored him. "At least he didn't ask about Chris. I'm so done discussing that douche." Bailey had briefly dated an NHL player who had since been embroiled in a penis Twitpic scandal.

"Gabby's on the case. No questions about our personal lives, thank God." He pointed to the huge sign denoting the shuttle to the Athletes' Village. "Not that I don't really enjoy clarifying for the millionth time that no, we're not a couple off the ice, and dancing around the fact that I'm a complete homo without actually saying or denying it."

She smirked. "We're totally their *favorite* team. You know the Feds wish we would just pretend to date each other so people will stop asking and we could be part of their perfect little hetero fantasy."

Bailey had started referring to the United States Figure Skating Federation by the nickname after they were subjected to three days of media training a few years ago and it was made very clear that Dev and Bailey were to uphold a certain image and basically never tell the truth to the press. Instead they told versions of the truth, carefully sanitized.

By the time they climbed off the shuttle by the sprawling collection of buildings that comprised the Athletes' Village, Dev's energy was flagging. It was going to be a very long day, but he couldn't give in to the jet lag and mess up his training. Olympic officials checked their credentials carefully and ushered them to their apartment block. Dev hoped the team had delivered their baggage as promised.

The American skaters were paired together, their rooms peppered in the same hallway along with some other American athletes. Bailey's roommate, an ice dancer named Shelby, squealed as she opened the door, and Dev left them to their excitement. He was rooming with Andrew, who was fast asleep atop his Olympic duvet, snoring softly and still wearing the team jacket, a variation on a pea coat featuring red and white accents on navy blue.

Dev didn't have the heart to wake him.

He inspected the neat room with its two single beds and cramped sitting area in the corner with four chairs, and a small flat-screen TV mounted on the wall. The window was almost half of the exterior wall, making the room bright and cheery. Annecy's Olympic colors were green and purple, and the room's accents, including the small table between the two beds, all featured those colors.

Dev hung up his clothing in half of the closet and unpacked his toiletries in the bathroom. He needed that shower, but first he needed caffeine. Leaving Andrew snoring for a little while longer, Dev made his way to the village's cavernous dining hall. Hundreds of long tables filled the center of the hall with seating for thousands. Food stations around the outside offered—what seemed at a glance—every kind of meal imaginable. Dev's stomach growled. Maybe he'd grab lunch too. Breakfast? He checked his phone. No, lunch.

First he followed the smell of brewing coffee to a cafe set up near the entrance. The hall was relatively empty, with clumps of people milling around and eating. Most athletes were arriving in the next few days, and it would soon be a madhouse. With his ID badge, everything was free, and Dev was extremely glad the pairs event was always first, because he'd have time after to treat himself. Until then, he had to stick to his diet. Lean protein, green vegetables, and a small amount of whole grains. He strode by the golden arches and whimpered as he breathed in the unmistakable scent of McDonald's grease. Sweet, sweet grease. How he missed it.

When he had his small black coffee in hand, he couldn't resist adding a packet of sugar. Or two. No one had to know.

Perhaps it was the caffeine, but Dev found himself buzzing with the Olympic spirit as he walked through the village. It hummed with new arrivals and palpable anticipation, and he grinned as he made his way back to his block. A young woman held the elevator for him, and he thanked her as he hurried inside. Jet lag be damned—he was at the Olympics and it was going to be *awesome.*

As the doors started to close, the woman stuck her arm out. "There's room!"

Then Mikhail Reznikov walked on.

Of course.

Dev couldn't seem to look away, and when their eyes met, heat rushed through his veins and straight to his groin. After a long moment, they both turned their heads. Dev hadn't seen him at all since the Grand Prix Final press conference. He'd refused to watch clips of Russian Nationals or Europeans on YouTube, even though Bailey and their coaches had wanted to check in on the competition.

No, he'd made sure the temporary insanity of Kyoto was completely worked out of his system. Now with one look at Mikhail, the lust was roaring through him.

Longest. Elevator. Ride. Ever.

When Dev finally escaped, he barreled into his room past a snoring Andrew. He barely made it into the shower before he had his cock in hand, jerking it desperately as memories of Mikhail's kisses and visions of his blue eyes and hard body took over his mind. Closing his eyes, he spread his legs and gave in.

Chapter Three

"**H**EY, MA."

"Aren't you awake yet? You sound tired."

Dev yawned and kicked at the duvet where his foot was caught in it. "I'm awake. Andrew's in the shower, so I'm just…resting my eyes until he's done."

His mother clucked her tongue. "I know how you rest your eyes, Devassy. Get your bottom out of bed. Are you practicing today?"

"Uh-huh." Dev closed his eyes again, cradling his cell between his cheek and the pillow. "There's a bus to the rink at Albertville."

"Why didn't they have the Olympics there again if they like the rink so much? You shouldn't have to go so far."

"It's only, like, an hour away, Ma. We don't get to have official practices at the rink in Annecy until a couple days before the event. Believe me, I'm happy to be out of the way with the team in Albertville while I get over the jet lag and settle in."

"Just do your best. You know we're proud of you no matter what. We wish we could be there. It's my fault that—"

"*Ma.* It's not your fault. You're just getting your balance back after that infection. As much as I want you to be here, I don't want you messing up your inner ear on the flight. You were in bed for a month. It's not worth the risk."

She sighed heavily. "It seems unfair. I wish Bailey's parents could have used our tickets."

"Me too, but it's been a tough couple of years for them with the layoff. Her mom's new job doesn't pay half what the old one did."

His mother tsked. "We would have paid for them to go, Devassy. We are all family. You know we love Bailey like she was our own. Such a good girl. So much better than that silly thing Felicia. I think of her because I saw her mother at the Target just the other day. We smiled and said nice things and pretended Felicia hadn't been very foolish to break up with you. She thought she would do so much better with that other boy, and where are they now? Nowhere. They didn't even make a world team before giving up." She harrumphed. "That's what she gets for thinking my son is not good enough for her."

Dev chuckled. "Ma, I'm glad she dumped me. You don't have to hold a grudge. It was six years ago."

"You're my only child, Devassy. I will always hold grudges in these cases."

He could hear her bangles jingling and could just imagine her waving her arm.

"But forget the past. Like I said, we wish the Robinsons had let us pay for France. It would be our pleasure."

Dev smiled, feeling a wave of affection for her. "I know, and they know it too. You guys have been so generous to me and Bailey over the years. But it's not just the tickets to the events, it's the flights and the hotel and food."

"Yes, yes, and we would pay!"

"That's too much. It's all good, Ma. I wish you were coming, but just think—you'll be able to watch on TV and criticize the commentators. You love that."

"They talk too much, Devassy, and sometimes they don't know a thing about what they are saying. I'll never forget when that Scott Hamilton had the nerve—"

"Ma. It's okay. Breathe. How's Dad? Is he in surgery?"

She changed gears again instantly, as she always did. His mother could rant about something one second and calmly ask about your day the next. "Yes, there was a pileup this morning and he was called in. Oh, did I tell you? Your cousin John was accepted to law school at Harvard. Early admittance. Very prestigious. He'll be living with us this summer while he finds an apartment. We thought he could use your room. Unless you'll be needing it."

Dev groaned. "Ma, could you give it a rest for five minutes? I can't think about that right now."

"I know, I know. I was just saying. Devassy, you've lived away for so long. We miss you."

His parents were the only people who still called him by his given name. Dev had learned very early that having the word "ass" in your name was like catnip to schoolyard bullies. He'd been just Dev ever since to the rest of the world. He sighed. "I miss you too. I really do. But I'm not sure what I'm going to do."

She tsked again. "Don't think about it now. Just focus on the Olympics," she said, as if she hadn't brought it up.

Dev could only laugh. His mother was never going to change, and he'd accepted it long ago. "I will."

"Oh and John Uncle booked a very good flight from Seattle in March."

"That's so nice that he and Susan Auntie would come for Worlds."

"Of course they will come! Everyone is coming. The Robinsons are driving from Pittsburgh and don't tell Bailey, but her brother is coming all the way from California. It will be a huge party at our house the night before the short program."

"Are you making biryani?" Dev's stomach growled at the thought of the spicy rice and chicken dish.

"Why do you ask silly questions, Devassy? Of course there will be biryani. And raita, *masala dosa, idli* and coconut chutney, and fish curry—and *meen* curry—and *vada*."

He groaned. "You have to make this party *after* the competition so I can gorge myself. I bet there will be mango pickles too."

"What are you saying? When do we not have mango pickles in this house? And naturally there will be a party after. Your retirement party. You didn't get a degree from college, so this will be your graduation."

Dev's lack of a college education could still be a controversial subject at times. While he'd done well in high school, skating had been his passion and college would have been too much of a distraction. He kept his tone even and quickly changed the subject. "Sounds good, Ma. I'd better get ready. Bailey will be here bright and early."

"Because she is a very smart girl. Be good. We love you!"

"Love you too. Bye." He tapped his phone to end the call. His mother had advised him to "be good" for as long as he could remember. He took a deep breath and jumped out of bed. Time for practice.

Time to be good.

"THERE'S SOMETHING YOU should know."

Dev and Bailey shared a glance as the rest of the team climbed off the small bus behind them. Louise was waiting on the sidewalk, rather grim faced, even for her. A few of the Feds milled around, looking intense. Dev raised an eyebrow. "Don't keep us in suspense, Lou."

"There was some kind of catastrophic electrical problem and fire at the rink down the street that did a lot of damage. No one was hurt, but the ice melted and they're not sure when the system will be fixed."

Bailey frowned and nodded to the sprawling arena behind Louise. "But our rink's okay, right?"

"Absolutely. But the organizers asked the federation if another team could use it this week too. They said yes. Olympic spirit and all that crap."

Dev's pulse spiked. "Which team?" *Anyone but the Russians. Anyone but the Russians. Anyone but—*

"The Russians."

Bailey groaned. "Seriously? So instead of private practice, this will be just as stressful as official practice all week. Minus the reporters and spectators, at least. But still. This is supposed to be our safe space. What's the point in paying all this money to rent a rink out of Annecy if we can't have privacy? I know, I know. No one planned this."

The Russians. Dev ran a hand through his hair. It felt like the universe was throwing Mikhail Reznikov into his path every chance it got. He was tense enough with the competition looming, and every time he saw Mikhail he didn't know whether to punch him or kiss him. Now he'd see him again today, and this jumble of emotions would only get more tangled and fucked-up.

"Dev? How are you feeling about this?" Louise asked.

"I don't know," he answered truthfully.

"You know what this is?" Louise asked. "It's a challenge, and you two are going to knock it out of the park. We're still going to have different practice times. Very segregated. When the US team is on the ice, they'll use the gym facilities, and vice versa."

"Yeah, but they'll be in the building. They can watch," Bailey noted.

"Both the federations agreed it will be strictly forbidden to go near the rink when it's not your scheduled practice time. This is a huge facility, and there's lot of room."

Dev glanced around at where the other skaters were receiving the news from their coaches. One of the federation officials tried to soothe an ice dancer. "It's all right for the guys. There hasn't been a Russian contender since Plushenko finally retired."

"I still don't believe it, by the way. He's going to show up when he's, like, fifty, and he'll still be landing quads," Bailey said.

Louise smirked, and Dev burst out laughing. With the tension broken, Dev shrugged. "It's fine. We'll do our thing, and they'll do theirs." *Please, universe. I'm begging you.*

"And if they're watching, we'll knock their socks off." Bailey grinned. "Come on. Let's get on the ice."

DEV SWORE LOUDLY as he skidded to a stop in the corner of the rink. "God damn motherfucking fuck!"

"You're not staying in the circle. Your right shoulder's dropping," Louise said from where she watched on the other side of the boards.

"I know!"

"Then stop doing it. *Now.*"

Their side-by-side triple toes shouldn't be a problem for him, but Dev couldn't land one to save his life. He brushed off his pants and reached for Bailey's hand as they circled the rink, dodging their teammates, engrossed in their own practices.

She squeezed his fingers. "It's just nerves."

"I never fall like this." Dev shook his head. Even though he knew the Russians weren't watching—all the curtains on the entrances to the seating were firmly closed—he felt as though Mikhail's eyes were on him, searing into his skin. Making him want to do things and feel things that were completely *insane.*

"Come on, let's do another lap." Bailey gave him a smile.

They stroked around the rink again, and Dev closed his eyes for a moment. He soaked in the familiar sensation of being on the ice with Bailey beside him. They moved as one with easy grace, which had taken time and many, many hours of practice to achieve.

I can do this. There's nothing else but me, Bailey, and the ice. Just another day at the rink.

"Relax. Let your body do what it's trained to do. Use your muscle memory," Louise called as they neared.

Dev breathed deeply as he separated from Bailey and they went into their three turns, changing direction back, front, and then back again as they used their toe picks to vault them into the air. Arms tight across his chest, Dev spun three times and landed smoothly on his outside edge, holding his free leg extended as he glided. Beside him, Bailey landed in perfect unison.

"That's it. Now again," Louise said. "Then we'll do a short program run-through. It's your turn for music."

Dev loved their short program. "Lux Aeterna" from the soundtrack to *Requiem for a Dream* had been used by other skaters in the past but not for several years. The propulsive score built dramatically, and Dev felt as if the orchestra was driving them onward, giving them energy and passion. They started with their triple twist—one of their best elements.

After they gathered speed, Bailey vaulted up with her toe pick as Dev snapped her up into the air above his head, bringing his hands almost all the way down to his sides while she rotated three times in a blur. He caught her by the waist in the air above his shoulders before placing her down on the ice. Sometimes she came down a little harder than others, but today she glided out of the catch and extended her leg as if it had been the easiest thing in the world.

Next were the side-by-side jumps, and they nailed them. They ticked off the other elements as they went—death spiral, step sequence, pair spin combination. Then it was time for the throw. As they skated around the corner of the rink, Dev drew Bailey in close with his hands on her waist. Their free legs extended in unison as they went into the three turn and he propelled her into a triple Salchow from her back inside edge. She spun in the air, tilting slightly as she came down and fought for the landing. She touched down with her hand, but didn't two foot.

"That's it. Muscle it out," Louise shouted as they skated by. "Stay strong."

Their last element was the lift. Each season there was a different style of lift required in the short program, and this year it was a hand-to-hand lift. He skated backward with Bailey facing him and took her hands.

"You got this," she said as she gripped him. Sometimes they talked to each other during programs. It really depended on the day, and there was no rhyme or reason.

Bending his knees deeply, Dev pressed her up above his head with his arms straight as he began rotating down the length of the ice. They changed positions as Dev grabbed her hip with one hand and Bailey extended her legs out into a star position, her upper body parallel to the ice. She still grasped his other hand but then let go and lifted her arm to complete the star. Dev extended his own arm, balancing her just on one arm while she held on to his shoulder with her free hand. To bring her down, he lowered her over his shoulder and she spun out of the lift.

With speed and vigor, they skated into their final position standing back to back. Louise clapped and nodded, and Dev raised his hand for a high five.

Bailey slapped his palm with a grin. "Let's do it again."

"THE NEXT BUS isn't for an hour. I'm going to go take a run around the arena before I hit the showers. See you in a bit," Bailey said before disappearing into the locker room.

It had been a long day, and Dev was more than ready to relax and let the steam soak up some of his aches and pains. He nodded to one of the Russian ice dancers as he walked into the locker room. Most of the skaters had caught the earlier bus, it seemed. Andrew glanced up as he finished lacing his sneakers.

"Hey, man. I was thinking about going for a run. You up for it?"

"No, but if you hurry, you can catch up with Bailey."

Andrew's face lit up. "Seriously? Later!" He disappeared so quickly he practically left a vapor trail.

The ice dancer chuckled. "So much energy," he said in a thick accent. "To be so young again."

"What are you, twenty-five?"

"*Da*. Feels like forty-five right now." He rubbed his lower back.

"I hear ya."

Dev unlaced his skates and stripped out of his simple black practice clothing. He pulled his flip-flops from his bag and grabbed a towel. The showers were down a short hallway. As he passed the door to the sauna, he saw a few skaters baking inside. The long shower room was divided into ten curtained stalls, with five on each side.

He headed toward the back and hung his towel on the hook beside the stall. There was one other shower running, but it stopped as Dev stood outside his stall, waiting for the water to reach the right temperature. He turned automatically when he heard the curtain sliding back.

Hand frozen in midair as he reached for his towel, Mikhail stood several feet away in the doorway of a stall on the other side of the room. Water dripped down his taut, lean body, and Dev couldn't stop from staring at Mikhail's long, uncut cock, hanging with his meaty balls. A trail of dark hair led down from his belly button to a neatly trimmed thatch. A small tattoo of a flying bird drawn with black lines—an eagle, perhaps?—adorned Mikhail's left hip.

What am I doing? Danger, Will Robinson! Danger!

Dev's throat was suddenly dry, and he forced his gaze back up. Mikhail's blue eyes were dark, and he licked his lips. The silence stretched taut between them. Then Mikhail moved, but instead of leaving, he shoved Dev back into the shower stall and under the warm water. Dev hit the wall and before he could even blink, Mikhail was on his knees, his hands like brands on Dev's hips.

Gone was the cool and collected competitor as Mikhail looked him up and down, eyes wild. It felt as if all the blood in Dev's body rushed to his dick, and he couldn't move—could barely breathe—as he waited to find out what happened next. What were they doing? They hated each other. They shouldn't want this. Yet Mikhail stared up at him hungrily as if waiting for permission.

Dev gripped Mikhail's hair, gasping as Mikhail swallowed his cock almost down to the root, one hand wrapped around the base as he hollowed his cheeks.

"Oh fuck," Dev whimpered. It was so hot and wet and *amazing*. Mikhail's lips stretched over him, and he stared up, completely open in a way Dev had never seen, not even during their madness in Kyoto. Everything Dev hated about Mikhail— his arrogance and cold perfection—was flung away in the messy, desperate sucking as he swallowed Dev fiercely.

All of Dev's defenses shattered, and he gave in. Fingers tangling in Mikhail's hair, he pumped his hips, unable to control himself. He was about to apologize, but Mikhail moaned softly and urged him on, opening his mouth wide, his hands loosening on Dev's hips. Eyes falling shut, he took Dev's thick cock eagerly as Dev rocked his hips and fucked Mikhail's mouth.

They should stop this. Someone could walk in at any moment. Good God, they were at the *Olympics!* Chest heaving, Dev pulled out, his dick smacking Mikhail's cheek. Dev opened his mouth to say something—anything!—that would bring them to their senses, but he could only stare at Mikhail's wet lips and raw, lust-darkened eyes.

Someone will find us!

But then, his eyes locked with Dev's, Mikhail teased the fore-skin and traced the throbbing vein on the underside of Dev's shaft with his tongue. Groaning, Dev reached blindly for the curtain and whipped it shut, unable to tear his eyes away from the man at his feet.

He finally had Mikhail Reznikov on his knees, and he'd never imagined it would be like this.

Okay, maybe he *had*, but it was so much better than his deep-est fantasies—the ones he hadn't wanted to acknowledge even to himself. Mikhail's cheeks were flushed, water dripping over his pale skin in the steamy shower, and he was all beautiful abandon, free and hot-blooded the way he'd never seemed on the ice.

Mikhail took over sucking Dev greedily again, his fingers teasing along Dev's crack. It was so hot, and Dev wanted to cry out, but pressed his lips together with a whimper. "Don't stop," he whispered.

As he took in every inch, Mikhail jerked his own cock, and Dev imagined what it would be like to touch Mikhail himself, to taste him and swallow him to the root, to bury his face in Mikhail's ass and fuck him with his tongue and get him ready for more. He wondered how Mikhail liked it and how tight his ass would be and whether he'd let Dev inside.

At the thought, Dev stifled a cry, and Mikhail sucked even harder. When he fondled Dev's balls, it was all over. Dev tried to warn him and push his head away, but Mikhail wouldn't move. The pleasure was a tidal wave, and Dev banged his head on the slick wall as he shook with the power of his release.

Mikhail swallowed repeatedly as Dev shot his load, milking him until it dribbled down his chin and he pulled off with a dirty *pop*. Before Dev could put a thought together, Mikhail was jacking himself off furiously. He came with a breathy moan, shuddering.

Dev's knees were weak. He closed his eyes and breathed deeply. When he opened them, he realized that, yes, he was in fact in a public shower with his sworn enemy panting at his feet. Mikhail sat back on his heels and rested his head against Dev's hip. He looked up, his face soft and vulnerable. He seemed so much younger suddenly.

Before Dev knew what he was doing, he caressed Mikhail's hair. He was struck with the urge to take Mikhail to bed and hold him close, to curl around him and kiss him until they slept. Sighing, Mikhail leaned into Dev's touch and murmured something in Russian before pressing a kiss to Dev's inner thigh.

Oh my God, I've lost my mind. It's official. I'm insane.

Dev swallowed hard. "Um. I don't...we..." He cleared his throat. "Mikhail..."

"Misha."

"What?"

He got to his feet and stared at Dev intently. "Misha. This is what friends call me."

"I'm not your friend." Dev was simply stating a fact.

Mikhail—*Misha*—smiled softly. "No. You are my...little rebellion." He pressed their lips together gently. "Thank you for that."

"I...you're welcome? We shouldn't...we can't." *But I don't ever want to stop.*

Mikhail's expression clouded. "No. We can't." He leaned their foreheads together. "But it felt good, yes?" he whispered.

Then he was gone, the plastic curtain waving in his wake.

Dev stood under the water and closed his eyes.

Yes.

Chapter Four

"**E**XPLAIN TO ME why you didn't take a shower at the rink? *Again?* Because this is an hour-long bus ride, and you stink." Bailey curled her lip.

"I didn't feel like it." Dev knew it was a lame answer, but he couldn't tell her the truth. On the ice, he could shut off his mind and stay focused. But as soon as he stepped off the rink, he was anxious and on edge, desperate to see Misha again. Even though he knew how dangerous it was. If people found out, it would affect Bailey's career as well. The Feds would lose their collective shit, for starters. Dev had been so reckless twice now, and he didn't trust himself even a little.

"Why are you such a grump? We had a good practice."

He sighed. "I'm just tired. I'm sorry. It's not you." His stomach churned. He hated not telling Bailey what was really going on. She was always the person he'd go to with a problem. But he couldn't tell her about Misha. Not now, right before the biggest competition of their lives. It was his job to protect her, and he had to protect her from the truth until after the event.

"Duh. Of course not. I'm practically perfect in every way. It couldn't be me."

Dev chuckled and pressed a kiss to her cheek. "It's true. I have the perfect partner."

"*Yeah* you do." She kissed him back. "And she's going to leave you to your broody man-thoughts and go gossip with Shelby. I hear there is *drama* in the Canadian camp. It's always the quiet ones."

Dev watched the dark countryside go by, the imposing Alps gleaming in the moonlight and dominating the landscape. He needed to get it together and forget about what happened. On the ice, he was able to shut off his brain and throw himself into practice. At this point, they were so well trained and he could do the programs with his eyes closed. He breathed through every movement, letting them take over his mind and body completely.

But once he left the rink, his brain flew into overdrive with a whirl of conflicting thoughts and feelings. Confusion. Curiosity. *Lust.* Dev had been with his fair share of men over the years and had a few relationships, but he'd never experienced anything like this before. He knew it was pathetic to hustle from the locker room as if he was afraid of Misha, but he was terrified of his own weakness.

Misha. He'd tried to fight it, but Dev found now that he couldn't think of him as Mikhail. It was such a forbidding, formal-sounding name—which had fit perfectly when he'd been Dev's hated rival. But the needy, passionate man on his knees in the shower, with his pupils blown and lips swollen? That was Misha.

It was as if Dev saw him for the first time. It wasn't only the mind-blowing sex. Dev found himself wondering what Misha was really like. He'd seemed so vulnerable afterward, resting his head against Dev's thigh, laid utterly bare in more ways than simply being undressed. He was commanding and austere on the ice, but he'd willingly fallen to his knees and taken everything Dev could give him as if he needed it like oxygen.

For the past few years, Mikhail had been more of an idea than a man—the perfect machine that Dev and Bailey had to conquer to win. Dev could admit that technically, Kostina/Reznikov were exquisite. The height of their throws and twists, their speed and unison—they made it all look so effortless. Yet Dev had always found their skating cold and impersonal. Soulless.

But now he'd glimpsed Misha's soul in his guileless eyes as he'd submitted so eagerly to Dev. Where Dev had once thought him impossibly shallow, now it felt as if there were oceans there beneath the surface. Dev was consumed with the need to discover more. Discover everything.

He sighed and leaned his forehead against the cool window. The memory of Misha kissing him so sweetly filled his head—the softness of his lips and scrape of his five-o'clock shadow against Dev's thigh. His final whisper echoed in Dev's mind. It *had* felt so good, and he longed to feel it again. To explore further and lose himself.

But more than that, he wanted to see Misha smile again. He couldn't recall if he'd ever heard him laugh, although he must have at some point, surely. What kind of movies did Misha like? What kind of food? What did he like to do off the ice?

Dev groaned softly. It was official. He didn't just want to have sex with Misha again. He wanted to go on a *date*.

AFTER DINNER IN the buzzing dining hall, Dev left Bailey—still gossiping, and he had to admit he'd really enjoyed the story about the dressing room diva throwdown after one of the Canadian women cut the other off just before a jump in practice. He returned to the apartment block, and as he walked into the lobby, his heart skipped a beat.

Looking long and lean and utterly *fuckable* in jeans and a Henley, Misha leaned against the wall near a seating area, tapping at his phone. He glanced up as the door closed behind Dev with a soft *thud*. When he met Misha's hungry gaze, Dev's pulse rocketed. He stopped in his tracks. Should he go over? Should he run to the elevators? *Should I slap myself because I'm acting like a teenage girl?*

Without a word, Misha turned and headed for the two elevators on the far side of the lobby. He pressed the button.

Dev's feet moved, and a moment later he stood next to Misha, watching the numbers tick down as one of the elevators neared. There was a foot between them, but Dev could feel an electric heat skittering over his skin. A few other people fell in behind them as they boarded the elevator. When Dev moved to press the button for his floor, Misha caught his wrist before Dev could raise it. His touch burned, and Dev glanced at him, but his face was impassive. Keeping his gaze forward, Misha raised his other hand and slowly, with purpose, pressed the button for his floor.

Dev's breath stuttered.

Get off on my floor. Press the button now before it's too late. Press it. Press it!

Dev watched his floor go by without any regret. Anticipation roared through his body and his heart pounded as he followed Misha off the elevator and down the hall. He held his breath, hoping they wouldn't run into anyone who knew them. Misha's teammates were all likely housed nearby, and if they saw them—

But they didn't, and a moment later they were inside Misha's room with the door closed. It was identical to Dev's, but on the opposite side of the building. Dev leaned back against the door. It was dark in the room, but the blind was up, and moonlight cast them in a silvery glow. Misha stood by the far bed near the window, watching Dev silently.

"Your roommate…"

"Gone to dinner with his girlfriend. Spending the night at her hotel."

"Oh." Dev was breathing shallowly. "Okay."

Misha peeled off the Henley and popped the button on his

jeans. "Okay," he repeated.

Dev wanted to lick Misha's dark nipples and run his hands across his broad chest, down to his cut abs and lower. There was nothing left to say. Pulse thundering, he closed the distance between them and took Misha's head in his hands. He traced Misha's lips with his thumb, and Misha opened his mouth and sucked it in slowly.

They kissed deliberately, exploring each other's mouths, hands roaming until the need was too much and Dev had to be naked. Evidently Misha felt the same, and he tore at Dev's shirt and ripped it over his head before rubbing their chests together.

Both moaning, they stripped off the rest of their clothes in a fevered rush, kissing and touching and grinding against each other like dogs in heat. Dev was going to get off soon just like that, standing there by the bed, but then Misha broke free and snatched a small bottle of lube off the bedside table. A box of condoms sat there as well, and Dev realized Misha had prepared for this—had waited in the lobby and enticed Dev back to his room.

Dev's stomach clenched. He wasn't sure how to feel. Angry? Flattered? Was this all a game? Was he being played? He searched Misha's gaze and found only heat and longing there, open desire in his parted lips as Misha slicked his long fingers and climbed on the bed.

As Misha moved onto his hands and knees, Dev stared, mesmerized. The lean muscles in Misha's back and arms gleamed in the moonlight, his thighs flexing as he reached back with his right hand to spread his round ass. His hole exposed, he started fucking himself, a breathy moan escaping his lips. He looked over his shoulder to where Dev stood, frozen.

If this was a game, Dev couldn't do anything but play.

Dick throbbing, he knelt behind Misha on the narrow bed and slicked his own fingers before knocking Misha's away. Misha cried out as Dev pushed two fingers inside. Misha's hole was shockingly tight, and Dev removed one of his fingers.

"*Nyet.* I want it. Fuck me hard. I have no patience."

He didn't want to hurt Misha—he truly didn't, he was surprised to realize—but Dev was rock hard, and his own patience was in short supply. "You sure?"

Misha pushed back with his ass. "Da, da. I want your cock."

Desire thrumming through him, Dev shoved his second finger back into the grasping heat before adding a third. "Fuck, you're tight," he muttered. For the first time Dev understood the appeal of fisting. He wanted to reach all the way inside and possess Misha.

On his elbows now, Misha moaned and rocked his hips back. His usually perfect hair was a mess, and he panted with his mouth open as he turned his cheek to the mattress. He was always so controlled on the ice, but here he was unrestrained and radiant, and Dev was transfixed.

Misha reached for the side table and nearly knocked the box of condoms over before he pulled out a string of foil packets and tossed them at Dev, whapping him in the face. Dev didn't want to take his fingers out of Misha, but the reminder that his cock would go in next was enough incentive. Hands shaking, it took three tries for Dev to get one open. He rolled on the condom and squirted it with extra lube. His throat was dry as he gripped Misha's hips and inched inside.

Little gasps escaped Misha's lips, and Dev pressed soothing openmouthed kisses to his spine. "Okay?"

"*Porasitel'no,*" he murmured.

Dev forced himself to stop moving. "What?"

"Amazing. It burns beautifully. Go on." Misha bore down, sweat beading on his back as he worked to let Dev into his body.

His heat gripped Dev's cock, and Dev breathed deeply to control himself, wondering when Misha had last had sex, considering how tight he was. At the thought of Misha on his hands and knees for someone else, jealously flared. With one hand on Misha's shoulder, Dev thrust his hips. Misha's ass stretched tight as he filled him, and he pulled out a few inches to admire the view of his dick in Misha's sweet, pale ass before he slammed in deeper. Misha urged him on with soft cries and pleas to fuck him harder, harder, *harder*. For someone so quiet in the dressing room over the years, Misha was vocal in bed, alternating Russian and English as he moaned.

"Da. Yes, yes—like that. *Eshe.*"

Lips parted, Dev worked Misha's ass. Their flesh slapped together, loud with their pants and groans in the small room. Misha was down on his chest now, head to the side and hands clutching the sheets. Dev thought of him on the top of the podium, imperious and untouchable. Now Misha was bent over for Dev, needing his cock.

Dev held him down by the back of his neck as he leaned over and angled in deeper, his hips snapping as he pounded Misha harder.

"*Pozhaluysta*. Pozhaluysta," Misha begged. *Please.*

Balls tightening, Dev slowed for a few moments, schooling himself as Misha whimpered. Dev wasn't going to be the one to break first. *This is one competition I'll win.* Thrusting again, he grunted as he pulled Misha's hair, lifting him up from the mattress onto his elbows. He slapped Misha's ass. Once, twice—

Misha reached down and stroked his cock with a desperate cry, his eyes closed and sweat dampening the back of his hair. He shuddered as he came, his tight ass clamping around Dev, as he growled something hoarsely in Russian. Dev's hips stuttered in short little thrusts as he let go, his orgasm ripping through his body like a tornado. He swore he actually saw stars as the white-hot bliss seared him.

Gasping for air, he collapsed on top of Misha in a heap of sweaty limbs. He never thought he'd see Misha so undone, and he reveled in it—in the fact that Misha had surrendered to him so beautifully. They were both flushed and sweaty and Dev felt the way he did after a perfect run-through. *Victorious.*

Finally he forced himself to move to get rid of the condom in the bathroom. By the light of the moon, he tossed it in the trash and hesitated as he stared at himself in the mirror.

I should get out of here. Wham, bam—it's been fun. Catch you later. Do svidaniya. They'd had their fun, and he should sneak back to his own room. Get a good night's sleep. Focus on his job. The opening ceremony was in three days, and tomorrow they'd start official practices with everyone watching. He should distance himself from Misha now. After all, he'd had him. What more did he want?

But as he watched his reflection, the thought of leaving filled him with shame. He wet a washcloth, hesitating by the bathroom door, suddenly uncertain. Perhaps Misha didn't even want him to stay and he was presuming too much. But Misha had rolled onto his back, and he waited with a small smile and beckoning hand. Dev cleaned him off and tossed the cloth back into the bathroom.

There was hardly room for one of them on the single bed, so Dev could only sprawl over Misha's body. Their legs entwined, he rested his head on Misha's chest, the hair there tickling his cheek in a way that made him smile. He closed his eyes as Misha played idly with Dev's short curls.

"You know, if you'd asked me before all this, I wouldn't have pegged you for a bottom. I wouldn't even have pegged you as gay," Dev said. He felt utterly relaxed and loose-tongued, even though he should go back to his room and never look back.

Misha's chest moved as he chuckled. "Oh yes, I love being fucked."

"Works out well, since I love doing the fucking."

"Have you tried the other way?"

"A few times. There's just something about plowing into a

tight ass."

"And I feel there is something about being...what did you say? Plowed. Perhaps it is because so much in my life is...hidden. Controlled. To give myself over and let go—I find no shame in it. Only pleasure." He rubbed his foot over Dev's calf. "Especially with you. You are excellent at fucking."

Dev smiled and caressed Misha's stomach, his fingers ghosting over Misha's soft cock. "The feeling's mutual." Not that they should be having any feelings whatsoever. Dev pushed the thought away.

"Where will you live? Once this is all over. You are retiring, yes?"

"Yes. I'm not sure where I'll settle down. After the show tours, I'll pack up my apartment in Colorado Springs. I'll go home to Boston for a visit. My family wants me to come back for good, of course."

"Boston is a good place."

"It is. I'm just...I don't know. I'm not sure. I have to figure out what I want my life to look like once I'm not competing. It's hard to imagine."

Misha sighed. "I imagine every day. I will return to America. Perhaps California this time. I would like to live by the beach. I will have a dog and walk for miles with my toes in the sand."

"If you love America, why did you go back to Russia after the last Olympics?"

His fingers stilled in Dev's hair. "I was given no choice. We failed to win gold and return honor to our country. Our bronze medal was nothing. Twice now, non-Russian pair has won gold. It is matter of great embarrassment. They brought us home to monitor training. Make sure we work harder and win this time."

Dev shifted and propped his head on his hand. "But how could they do that? It sounds like the Soviet era all over again."

"Yes. It gets worse and worse. They..." Eyebrows drawn,

Misha stared at the ceiling.

"What?" Dev caressed Misha's chest while a little voice in his head screamed. It was bad enough they were fucking—now they were *talking*? It should have been utterly surreal to lie in bed with Mikhail Reznikov, the ice king, but it felt strangely natural. Strangely right. He silenced the voice. "You can tell me."

Misha's gaze, still distant, became wistful. "I had a boyfriend in Connecticut. An accountant. David. We met in a bar one night. It was wonderful to go out in America, where no one knew me. He barely understood what figure skating was. In Russia, it is different."

"So what happened?"

"They found out. Had many pictures."

"How? They followed you?"

"Of course." He shrugged.

"Who? Like, the KGB?"

Misha smiled slightly. "Now it is FSB. *Federal'naya Sluzhba Bezopasnosti.* Federal Security Service. But yes, even with a new name they are same old KGB. The SVR spy for them overseas."

"The what?"

"*Sluzhba Vneshney Razvedki.*" Misha paused. "It would translate as foreign intelligence. They all do what they want with no laws to stop them. We are powerless."

"But…that's insane! Russia's still a democracy."

Misha snorted and met Dev's gaze. "That is big joke. They say democracy to the world but at home control everything. Everyone."

"What happened? They blackmailed you?"

"You know of the antigay laws, yes?"

"Of course. The total human rights violations? Scary shit."

"It would have been very bad for my family, if people knew about me. They told us we were to come back to Moscow. 'Russians should be in Russia,' they said."

"Jesus. That's terrible. I can't imagine. I mean, Bailey and I complain about the Feds being too controlling, but they're just an occasional inconvenience."

Misha's brow furrowed. "Feds? I thought...FBI are Feds? They are controlling you?"

"No, no. It's our nickname for our skating federation. They can be nosy as hell sometimes, and we had to kiss a lot of ass before we started winning, but it's nothing, really. I can't believe Russia's doing that to you. You must hate them."

"Government, yes. Leader who is dictator, yes. But my country I still love. Always. Government is destroying many good things. Beautiful things about my country are going away now. My father says it's like communism without..." He seemed to be searching for the right word. "Without ideals. Not for the greater good this time. For the good of those in power. Not the people."

"Was Kisa pissed about going back?"

"She told them we wouldn't go. She knew what David meant to me." He stared at the ceiling again. "Kisa is from the east. With our prize money, she was able to buy her family a new house. Her skating changed everything for them. When her mother became sick the year before, officials made sure she was able to see the specialist in Novosibirsk. That night, after Kisa refused to go, she came to my apartment very late. She wept, and I knew what they had done."

Dev's stomach twisted. "If you guys didn't go back, no more specialist for her mother." *God.* No matter how much the federation might get on his nerves sometimes, it would never be like that. "You know, I don't think I've ever seen Kisa cry once."

Misha's lips quirked into a smile. "Everyone thinks she is quite a bitch."

"Well..." Dev couldn't deny it.

Misha winked at him. "She is very tough. This is true. But she's really very shy. She is devoted to her family—she only agreed to train in Connecticut because Vasily was there. He is a wonderful coach. For many years he has been there now, and they could not make him return. He said he's an old man with no family left to threaten him with." Misha smiled again. "I miss him. Irina is an excellent coach, and we are very fortunate to have her, but with Vasily…" He paused. "We share the same humor."

"So, what's it been like the last four years in Moscow? Have they been spying on you?"

"I'm sure. But without boyfriends, there was nothing to distract me from skating. I put everything into training."

"What about David? Do you talk to him?"

Misha smiled sadly. "It was best for him to move on. I see online that he is married now. I cannot imagine such freedom—men marrying men and women marrying women. It is a glorious thing, to be so free. I hope for such acceptance one day."

Although it hadn't been that many years since marriage equality had been passed in some of the states, Dev was acutely aware that he already took it for granted. "Okay, no boyfriends in Moscow, but what about when you traveled for competitions? Surely they didn't follow you all the time."

"The problem with FSB is that you never know when they are watching. Better to assume it is always."

"Well, if they're watching right now, I hope they enjoyed the show."

Misha laughed. "I think we are safe here. Even so, it's too late now. Competition is next week. What can they do?"

A horrifying thought entered Dev's mind. "Wait—if they've been watching you…have you been celibate the past *four years?*"

Misha nodded. "Until Kyoto. I kept my secret self locked away, but you found the key." He brushed his thumb across Dev's bottom lip. "Sometimes I wondered what it would be like with you, but I never thought…"

"You wondered about me?" It was flattering, and Dev's stomach flip-flopped foolishly. *Get it together.*

"Of course. You are beautiful." Misha traced Dev's cheekbone with his fingertips.

He flushed. "Thank you. You know you're gorgeous, right?"

Misha shrugged. "Yes, but you have such love on the ice. Love for skating. It shines from you. I watch you and wish I could feel such joy. I confess it also made me angry sometimes."

Dev frowned. "But you love skating too."

"Once, yes. Very much." He sighed. "Then we moved back to Russia and everything changed. It does not lift my heart to skate any longer. You live and breathe it because you love it. For me it is a burden around my neck. A heavy thing. If we do not win…" He shook his head. "Russia becomes more and more like in the old days. I do not know what will happen if we shame the motherland like this. I pray I will not find out."

The instinct in Dev to insist that he and Bailey would win warred with his sympathy for the pressure Misha and Kisa were under. If he and Bailey lost, it would be a disappointment to their country, but one soon enough forgotten, especially considering how skating struggled to retain viewers in non-Olympic years. "What happens to your families now if you come back to the States after the Games?"

"Kisa will return to Russia. There is a boy from her town she will marry. Alexei. A man now, but he has waited."

Kisa Kostina with a secret childhood sweetheart? Dev had honestly never thought about her as anything but an impeccably French-manicured, bedazzled dragon lady. "What about your family? Do they know?" Dev swept his arm over their entwined bodies. "About you?"

"Yes. I thought I hid it well, but my father says he knew long ago."

"You definitely hide it well. I didn't have a clue."

Misha tapped Dev's nose. "I knew about you. There was just

something."

"I may not be officially out, but it's not exactly a state secret."

"And your family?"

"At first it was…an adjustment. I told my parents after high school. They didn't know what to be more shocked and disappointed about—that I was gay, or that I wasn't going to university. But they accepted it pretty quickly. My mom's tried to fix me up with pretty much every Indian lawyer and doctor in America at this point."

"You did not want this?"

Dev shrugged. "I've never really had time for anything serious. Most guys can't understand the dedication it takes to be a champion. And it's just been easier to keep it on the backburner. In skating I played straight the first few years, but then I just didn't say anything one way or the other. The Feds would have flipped if I admitted it, but at least they didn't start *stalking* me. Will anything happen to your family if you don't go back?"

Misha sighed. "My parents say they are too old to leave their home. They insist that I go to America, and that they will be fine." He blew out a long breath. "I do not know what will become of it, but I cannot stay in Russia. At least they have not closed the borders. I will have done my duty and they'll have someone else to worry about. When we win this gold, I will be free."

Dev clenched his jaw. Misha said it like it was a given, and Dev wanted that gold just as much. Granted, his freedom wasn't on the line, and he couldn't imagine the unfair strain on Misha. But what the hell was he doing in bed with the man who stood between him and his dream? What the hell was he doing feeling bad for Misha?

Maybe this is all part of the game.

He pulled away. "I should go. Your roommate might come back and—"

"No, no." Misha cupped Dev's face. "Let us not talk of medals or winning. We will do our best, and the judges will decide. Forget about competition when we are together."

Shaking his head, Dev untangled himself and turned to sit on the edge of the bed. "How can we forget about competition? This is crazy." He glanced over his shoulder at Misha, splayed out and utterly debauched. *So beautiful.* He fought the urge to touch him again. "We've both lost our minds. You realize this, don't you? This won't be like Salt Lake City. Only one of us can win. We shouldn't even be talking to each other, let alone…"

Misha skimmed his fingers over Dev's back. "Perhaps crazy. But I want your cock in me again and again. I dream of it since Kyoto." He sat up and moved behind Dev, wrapping his arms around him as he whispered in his ear. "I dream of you filling me up until it overflows and drips out of me. Then I take you in my mouth and make you come again, and I swallow it all. Every night I am spread open for you and—"

Groaning, Dev turned his head to take Misha's mouth in a kiss. Cock twitching, all other thoughts vanished from his mind as he pressed Misha back to the mattress. He tasted Misha's skin, traveling down his body with openmouthed kisses, licking his nipples and teasing the sensitive flesh. Misha sighed, arching up and holding tight to Dev's hair. Lower, Dev kissed the wings of the small eagle taking flight over Misha's hipbone. Misha spread his long legs wantonly, and God, he was *breathtaking*, offering himself up so freely.

Dev licked up and down Misha's cock and nuzzled his balls, but it was Misha's ass he wanted again. He pushed Misha's knees up farther and spread his cheeks before diving in. He buried his face in Misha's ass, licking at his hole and opening him up. He spit and pushed his tongue inside, and Misha cried out, his limbs twitching.

Reveling in the musky taste, Dev lost time fucking Misha with his tongue. When he glanced up, Misha was breathing with his mouth open, his skin flushed and head thrown back, revealing the length of his neck and the angle of his chin. Dev reached up and slipped two fingers into Misha's mouth. Misha sucked them eagerly, little moans escaping. With his fingers wet, Dev squeezed them into Misha's ass.

With tongue and fingers, he fucked Misha until Misha was panting, his leaking cock straining against his stomach.

"Pozhaluysta," he moaned.

Dev reached blindly for the condoms. He didn't bother with more lube, letting his saliva slick the way as he thrust inside Misha's ass. Gasping, Misha drew his legs up even farther, and his ankles were almost behind his head as Dev pounded into him.

"So tight. Fuck, you're so hot. So good," Dev muttered.

Misha squeezed around him, and his fingers dug into Dev's hips, urging him on harder and faster. He reached one hand into Dev's hair and yanked him down for a kiss, their tongues meeting as they moaned into each other's mouths.

"Fuck. Yes, yes—*fuck*." He reached for Misha's cock between them and stroked it in time with the motion of his hips as he plowed Misha's ass, stretching him and going deeper.

When he hit the right spot, Misha's whole body stiffened and vibrated, and then he came between them with a wordless cry. As he pulsed with his release, his ass convulsed around Dev's cock, and Dev drove into him desperately. He was so close to the edge, and he grunted as he slammed in and out. He knew Misha must be sore, but Misha urged him on, fingers tightening in Dev's hair.

"Yes. Come for me now. Fill me up," he commanded.

With a groan, Dev's orgasm rushed through him from his balls to the tips of his toes, the warmth incredibly intense as he jerked and gave Misha every last spurt. Even though he wore a condom, he imagined they were doing it raw.

As they came back down, Misha pressed soft kisses to Dev's face. "*Spasibo*," he whispered.

Dev closed his eyes and let himself forget about the real world.

Chapter Five

A S THE ELEVATOR doors opened, Dev held his breath. The hallway was empty, and he exhaled and hurried to his room. He was about to say a prayer to God, the universe or any omniscient being that happened to be listening when he heard the other elevator arrive, and Bailey's distinctive laugh ring out. He sighed. *So close.*

"Hey, partner!" Bailey called. She wore her running gear, and her auburn hair was pulled back in a ponytail. She said goodnight to Shelby, who disappeared into their room. As Bailey got closer, her eyes took on a familiar gleam. "Well, well, well. What do we have here? It's past ten, so we're both burning the midnight oil and Louise will kick our butts tomorrow even though our practice time isn't until later." She stopped in front of him, and a wicked smile lifted her lips. "But I've been doing laps with Shelby, and you? Hmm, let's see."

"Bailey, it's late. We should get to bed." He tried to duck by her.

She slapped his arm lightly. "Not before you tell me who you fucked!" She held up her hand. "Don't try to deny it. We both know that I can always tell. I'm glad you took my advice. Now you'll be relaxed and ready to go as we defy the odds and win gold with the best two performances of our lives. Come on, spill."

"I..." Looking into her excited, open face, Dev was struck with a wave of affection. He hated lying to her, but the truth about Misha right now would distract her and cause friction between them. His mind scrambled for a sport—any sport. Bobsled. It would do. "It was—"

The stairwell door ten feet away swung open, and Misha appeared. He froze, the proverbial deer in headlights as Dev's heart thumped so loudly he was certain Bailey would hear.

A furrow appeared between her brows. "Hey, Mikhail. How's it going?"

Misha didn't answer, still motionless, his eyes locked on Dev. Dev stared back as he tried desperately to think of something to say while Bailey glanced between them.

Her smile grew uncertain. "What's up? You guys both look guilty as hell. Did you—" She broke off, shaking her head and holding her hands up. "Wait, wait. What's happening? You didn't…" She stared at Dev. "Am I going crazy?"

Wordlessly, Misha closed the distance and held out his hand. Dev's cell phone. Heart sinking and stomach knotting, Dev took it with a nod and slipped it in his pocket. Misha disappeared into the stairwell. Dev took a deep breath. "Bailey…"

She stared, mouth agape. It was possibly the first time he'd ever seen her speechless. A *ding* echoed in the hall, and a group of athletes poured off the elevator. Bailey snapped her jaw shut, pressing her lips together into a grim line. She stalked to Dev's room, and he followed.

Inside, Andrew glanced up from where he was flopped on the nearest bed, tapping his phone. "Hey, guys! I was…are you okay?"

Bailey pointed to the door. "Out."

"Whoa." Andrew tensed. "What happened?"

Her nostrils flared, and he scrambled to his feet and escaped into the hall, the door shutting behind him with a loud *click*. Bailey crossed her arms over her chest.

"I must be losing my mind, right? Is it the altitude? Everything's foggy. Because it seems like you just had sex with *Mikhail*

Reznikov."

"B, it wasn't... I mean..." Dev ran a hand through his hair.

"What the actual fuck, Dev? Are you kidding me? I know I told you to get laid, but for the record, I didn't mean with *him!* Of all people! I can't—" She shook her head. "I can't even process this. How? Why? *How?*"

"This is such a cliché, but it just happened. In Kyoto, we—"

"In Kyoto?" Her voice rose. "You fucked him in Kyoto? I don't even... I can't believe this." She rubbed her face. "Is this real life? Am I on drugs? Am I hallucinating?"

"I know it's insane. I know, believe me. After the long program we were in the dressing room and I was so pissed about the scores and I picked a fight with him. One second we were at each other's throats, and the next..."

She heaved a shuddering breath. "So that's why you were late for the press conference. Why you were so flustered."

Dev nodded.

Bailey put her head down and took another breath. Then another. And another. When she looked up, her eyes glistened, and her anger had dissolved. "This has been going on since then, and you didn't tell me?"

"I wanted to. So badly. I never thought anything else would happen. Not in a million years! I tried to put him out of my head, but when I saw him again it was just... I can't explain it. We can't keep our hands off each other. It's complete lunacy, I know. I wanted to tell you. I swear. Please, Bailey." He reached for her.

Bailey jerked back, shaking her head again. "No. I don't. I can't. I..." She sucked in a breath, and a tear slipped down her cheek. "You're the person I trust a hundred percent to always be there for me. To always be *honest*, even if it hurts. I just...I don't know what to do with this. I can't talk to you right now. I feel like I don't even know you. You *hate* him. He's a soulless robot."

"He's—" Dev bit down the urge to defend Misha. "Not what

we thought."

She sniffed and swiped her nose with the back of her hand. "That's great. I'm glad to hear it. Well, I'm going to bed, because I can't deal with this." She turned.

"Bailey, I know I fucked up. Please forgive me."

Bailey opened the door as more tears fell. "I will. But not tonight."

Dev had never hated himself more. All he could do was climb into bed and close his eyes, awash in guilt. Bailey was his best friend, and he'd feel the same way in her shoes.

When Andrew came back, he quietly flicked off the light, and didn't say a word.

BAILEY DIDN'T SEEM to be closer to forgiving Dev the next morning. Dev and Andrew, who had been conspicuously cheerful and hadn't mentioned the night before, found Bailey, Shelby, and a few other teammates at one of the long tables in the dining hall. The last thing Dev wanted was for everyone else to know there was an issue, and Bailey clearly felt the same way. She chatted with the others as if it was any other morning but didn't look at him once. He couldn't blame her.

They typically had one blowout fight a year, usually about something meaningless, and usually when they were exhausted and stressed. They never held grudges. But Bailey had never been hurt like this before. They'd made a pact their first year together to always tell the truth, even if it was ugly. Until now, Dev had never kept anything from her.

When Bailey left to go get ready, Andrew leaned in and whispered to Dev.

"Are you guys going to be okay?"

"Of course," Dev answered automatically. He sighed. "I hope

so."

"I mean, you guys are *bros*. Whatever you did, it must have been bad."

But so good. Dev smirked. "You mean you weren't eavesdropping from the hall last night?"

Andrew sat up straighter. "Dude, no way." He seemed genuinely offended.

"Sorry. I admit I might have. You're a good guy, Andrew. I'm glad you're my roommate."

"Hey, put in a good word for me with Bailey, and we're square." He waggled his eyebrows.

Dev had to laugh. "I think I'm the last person to be pleading your case right now."

"Good point. I'll have to put my seduction plan into motion."

"Good luck with that, and I don't need to know the details. Ever."

Andrew laughed and was then distracted by the arrival of one of his training mates, an ice dancer named Sean who obviously had the metabolism of a teenage boy—which he was, so Dev supposed it was fair—because his plate was heaped with bacon.

Dev pushed his bran cereal around in his bowl. They were two days from the opening ceremony and four days from the short program, and his partner wasn't talking to him. Yet as upset as he was about the rift with Bailey, Dev couldn't help but think about Misha. He scanned the dining hall, examining the throng of people and looking for the distinctive red jackets and Misha's shock of dark hair. Each time he thought he spotted him, his stomach flip-flopped and crushing disappointment followed.

Even if Dev did spot him, it wasn't like he could just run over and kiss him. Even though that was exactly what he wanted to do. He felt like a junkie jonesing for a fix. He needed more. He remembered Misha's laugh and the slightly crooked way he smiled and—

"Yo, Dev. Earth to Dev."

He blinked at Andrew. "Huh?"

"Sean was asking about the arena. You guys are going today, right?"

"Uh-huh. Yeah." Guilt barreled through him. How could he be sitting there thinking about his rival? This was the biggest competition of his life. Of Bailey's life. He needed to focus.

Today was their first official practice at the new *Arène Olympique*. Thanks to Dev and Bailey's silver and the second team's eighth-place finish at Worlds last year, the US had qualified three pair teams. They'd be sharing their practice session with the two teams from France, so their sessions would be sure to draw big crowds. Along with the public, there would be media, judges, and officials from the skating federations. All holding up a magnifying glass to the skaters on the ice.

Despite what anyone liked to think, the competition began now, and Dev had to be ready. He left the soggy remnants of his cereal and went to prepare.

Their practice group was scheduled for eleven fifteen a.m., and Bailey and Dev caught the shuttle to the arena with their pair teammates. While there was generally quite a bit of friction between the other two teams, since Bailey and Dev were so far ahead in the rankings, the other teams didn't really compete against them. It had been a given that, barring disaster, Bailey and Dev would capture their fourth national title in January. The battle for silver and bronze had been fierce, and even now the smiles were strained.

This worked out well for Dev and Bailey as they chatted with the other skaters and not each other, acting as a buffer between their teammates. Dev smiled and nodded but only half listened. Bailey had still barely looked at him, and his stomach churned. He'd need a bottle of antacids before this day was over. Why had he been so stupid? Getting involved with Misha was the worst mistake he'd ever made. He was at the Olympics. His partnership and competition had to be his top priority, no matter what.

Yet he couldn't get Misha out of his mind. The sex had been unreal, but it really was more than that. He'd never been so infatuated, even as a teenager crushing on his hot-ass history teacher. He was already desperate to see Misha again, to touch him and kiss him and *talk* with him. He wanted to know about Misha's childhood. He wanted to know how he started skating. He wanted to know everything.

"Dev, do you have any advice for today?"

Blinking, Dev smiled at little Caroline, a blonde teenager who lived up to her nickname of Sweet, as in the old Neil Diamond song. "Sorry?"

"This is your second Olympics. I'm so nervous I could puke." She glanced at her partner, Grant. "Don't worry. I won't."

Dev gave her arm a squeeze. "Just try to ignore all the people in the stands. Think of it as another day at practice. Another run-through. You're ready. You wouldn't be here if you weren't."

Truthfully, Dev thought Caroline and Grant had been over-marked at Nationals, but the other team favored to medal, North/Rodman, had had a terrible Grand Prix season and made two major mistakes in their long program. Their component scores had been far too low, and the judges sent them the message that they'd disappointed too many times. The federation had the choice to still name North/Rodman to the Olympic team, but everyone knew it wasn't going to happen, and third-place Caroline and Grant were in.

Grant raised his hand as the shuttle pulled in to the arena. "Go team!" He high-fived everyone in turn.

"If we start chanting USA, I don't think we'll be very popular." Bailey laughed.

A cluster of fans waited by the skaters' entrance, and Dev and Bailey gave Amaya and Reiko fond hugs and chatted with them and other fans before posing for pictures.

Bailey's smile faded as they entered the arena and went through security. Louise was waiting in the backstage area near the dressing rooms. She opened her arms. "Here we are. Olympic venue!" She frowned. "What's wrong?"

"Nothing!" Bailey and Dev chirped in unison.

She narrowed her eyes. "All right. Go get ready. We're on the ice in twenty."

Dev loitered in the dressing room as long as possible. Even for official practice, he and Bailey just wore their typical black spandex gear. While the ice dancers typically wore proper costumes in practice, the rest of the skaters went casual. He thought of Misha in his practice outfit and the way his pants clung to his muscular thighs. Then he thought of how those thighs trembled as he'd pounded Misha's ass, and the sweet sounds he'd made, and—

He marched to the bathroom and splashed cold water on his face. With five minutes to go, Dev made his way to the rink in his skates, his skate guards clomping on the hard floor.

By the entrance to the rink adjacent to the empty Kiss and Cry area, Bailey and Louise waited with the other US and French teams and their coaches. During the competition, they'd sit on the bench in the Kiss and Cry with cameras a few feet away capturing every emotion as they waited for their marks. After a good skate, the Kiss and Cry was a fun place to be. After a bad one, it was torture.

At the end of each official practice, teams acknowledged the audience before leaving the ice. Dev knew the Russian teams were in the practice session before them, and one of the younger teams was taking their bows.

And of course, Misha and Kisa were coming off the ice just as Dev walked up. Kisa brushed by him without a glance, but as Misha straightened up from putting on his skate guards, he looked straight at Dev. For a long moment, their eyes met, and then Dev tore his gaze away and stood by Louise and Bailey.

God, he wanted to run after Misha and pull him into the nearest dark corner. It was like an itch on his skin, the need to touch him again. To hear his voice and smell his musky scent and see his eyes light up in amusement and darken with desire.

Shoulders high and rigid, Bailey stared at the ice. Louise raised an eyebrow.

"Ready to go, Dev?"

"Yep."

As soon as the last team from the earlier practice left the ice, their group streamed on, their coaches by the boards to take their skate guards and offer tissues or water. Bailey was already halfway around the rink, stroking with purpose, when Dev skated after her. He did his own lap, which wasn't unusual. Part of practice was always skating apart. They often did their own warm-up. After a few more laps, Dev caught up and reached his hand out. Without looking, Bailey took it, just as she had a million times before.

The announcer gave the order of music, and Bailey and Dev were third. Each team was allotted one program run-through with music, with all teams electing to do their short programs in this practice. With five teams who weren't used to practicing together on the ice, they were like fish in a tank, weaving around each other and sometimes coming too close for comfort. Over the years there had been some nasty collisions in practice, and Dev was always wary.

Caroline and Grant were first up with their music, and Dev and Bailey made sure to give them the right of way as they skated through their short program. Not all teams did a complete run-through, instead choosing to practice only key sections, but Caroline and Grant went from top to bottom, as did Dev and Bailey.

"Want to do the throw?" Dev asked.

"Sure," Bailey answered. She had to look at him then, but she was all business.

As Dev predicted, the stands were fuller than a typical practice, with the home crowd cheering on the French teams. Of course as top contenders, he and Bailey were also heavily scrutinized, and Dev could feel the weight of thousands of eyes watching their every move. The judges would be watching very carefully.

After they practiced the throw in the far corner of the rink a few times, Bailey landing all of them except for one where she got too out of position in the air, they skated back to Louise for a drink and to get her notes.

She didn't waste time. "What's the problem?"

Dev glanced at Bailey, who jerked her shoulders in a shrug. "Nerves. We're fine."

"Really?" Louise leaned in over the boards, her voice quiet but powerful. "Because you're barely making eye contact out there. You're my no-drama team. This is not the time to have a meltdown."

"We won't," Dev assured her.

"All right. Go back out there and act like you like each other. Which you do, by the way. Whatever this is, get over it and move on. You've worked too hard for too long for the wheels to come off now. When your music comes on, you're going to do your program like it's Sunday night and this is the one that counts. The judges are watching, and they are taking note. Now go work on your twist. You're not trying the quad, so your triple has to be perfect. *Citius, altius, fortius!*" Louise loved quoting the Olympic motto of "higher, faster, stronger."

The rest of the practice went fairly well, save for Dev slipping off his landing edge on his triple toe during their run-through. At least Bailey was talking to him and meeting his gaze. But as soon as they left the ice, the tension returned.

At the shuttle stop outside the venue, Dev cleared this throat. "Bailey, I think—"

"Not here. When we're alone." She waved to Caroline as the others joined them.

The ride back to the Athletes' Village seemed to take forever. While the others went straight to the dining hall, Bailey tromped through the snow in her boots and led the way to an isolated part of the small park nestled in the village. She was tiny, but she was a force to be reckoned with, and Dev hated to upset her. It was a cold, overcast day that seemed to match their moods.

"Okay." Bailey took a deep breath and blew it out. The bobble on the top of her woolen hat wavered. "The shock is wearing off, and I just have to say some stuff and get it off my chest."

"Okay." Dev braced himself.

"I feel that you should have told me what was going on, even though I know you were in a tough spot. I concede that there was really no good way for me to find out you're screwing our chief rival. I understand why you didn't tell me, even though it really hurts my feelings."

"I'm so sorry. I never wanted to hurt you." Dev blinked rapidly as his throat tightened. "It's the last thing I wanted."

"I believe you." She swiped at her eyes with her Olympic ring mittens. "I just don't understand how it happened. He stands for everything we've been fighting against. He and Kisa are the bull's-eye we've been trying to hit for the past three years since everything came together and we started climbing the ranks. And maybe that's not fair, to make them the villains, but they've always been so remote, up on their pedestal of perfection, and every day in practice the thought of knocking them down has fueled us."

"I know. Believe me, I couldn't stand him. I..." Dev ran a hand through his hair. "I don't understand it any better than you."

She took another long breath, and it fogged in the wintry air. "We've worked so hard. And I know that figure skating isn't going to change. They can change the judging system all they want, but there will always be politics and bullshit scoring. But we've done everything we can to become the first American pair to win gold. Each season we've laid out our game plan and our goals and how to achieve them. We've been methodical and exact and we've given up a big part of our lives. And this wasn't in the game plan. That's hard for me."

"I know. You're right, and I'm sorry. I'm not going to see him again. I'm one hundred percent committed to you and reaching our goals."

Sniffling, she nodded. "Okay. It's over, and we're moving on."

"You know you're my best friend in the whole world. I hated lying to you."

Eyes moist, Bailey stepped close and reached up to wrap her arms around his neck. He lifted her off her feet, and she clung to him, her breath warm where her face pressed into his neck.

"You're my best friend too," she murmured.

When he put her down, she stepped back and fixed her hat. "Okay. That's that." She frowned. "Where are your gloves?"

"I forgot them in the dressing room."

With an artful roll of her eyes, Bailey slipped off her left mitten and gave it to him. He put it on and reached for her left hand with his right, clasping it tightly as they trudged back through the snow, fingers entwined.

IT WAS NEARLY seven o'clock when Dev made his way back to his building. He and Bailey had spent the afternoon kicking each other's asses in the gym, and now Dev was ready for an early night, his sushi dinner making him pleasantly full. He'd normally avoid carbs, but he'd earned a little white rice.

As he walked into the lobby, his pulse spiked. There stood Misha, in almost the exact same position as the night before.

Waiting.

Misha met his gaze intently, and for a moment, Dev wanted nothing more than to go with him and lose himself again.

No. Not this time.

With a shake of his head, Dev detoured to the stairwell and took the six flights at a run, half hoping Misha would follow. He didn't. Lying forlornly on his bed, staring at the door, Dev told himself it was a good thing. His head agreed, but he wasn't so sure about his heart.

Chapter Six

"ALL RIGHT, BOYS! Wakey-wakey, shakey-shakey."
Dev grinned as he rubbed a towel over his head.
"Morning, Bailey." Although they'd made up, he was still relieved
to see her back to her normal self.

Andrew bolted up in bed, eyes wide. He sputtered. "What?
Bailey! I…you can't just burst in without knocking! I could have
been naked." He pointed to Dev. "He *is* naked!"

Bailey waved her hand dismissively and flopped into one of
the visitor chairs. "I've seen it all before. When we were first
starting out, we used to share hotel rooms at competitions to save
money. My parents could barely afford to pay Louise, let alone all
the other costs. Besides, we spend hours every day touching each
other. I'm comfortable with Dev's junk."

"But…" Andrew trailed off.

"Would it make you feel better if I got dressed?" Dev asked
with a smile.

"Yes! It would." Andrew blushed and slumped back under the
covers.

"Okay, while Andrew clutches his pearls, let's discuss the fact
that today's the day. Or should I say, tonight's the night. Opening. Ceremony. We've got practice today, and then it's fun, fun,
fun tonight."

As Dev stepped into his boxer briefs, Andrew escaped to the

bathroom. Dev shook his head. "You're going to give that poor kid a heart attack."

"He's at the Olympics. He's playing with the big boys now. Speaking of which…" She leaned forward in the chair, elbows on her knees as she lowered her voice. "There's something else I need to know about your little dalliance. Now, knowing you the way I do, I have one question. Is Mikhail Reznikov a *bottom*?"

It was Dev's turn to blush, and heat shot through him as memories filled his brain—Misha on his hands and knees, the feel of his tight ass, his ankles up to his ears as Dev pounded him—

"Wow." Bailey whistled. "He must be *quite* a bottom."

The shower was running now, but Dev sat on the chair next to Bailey and kept his voice down. "I could write songs about his ass."

Bailey's eyes widened and she grinned. "I never would have thought. I never even thought he played for your team."

"Me either! But he does. He really, *really* does."

"I'm torn between wanting every single detail and wanting to bleach my brain at the thought of you with him. He's just so…so…I mean, obviously he's gorgeous. I have eyes. But he's always seemed so uptight."

"I know. But Misha's not like that at all when you get to know him."

Her eyebrows shot up. "It's *Misha* now, is it?" She sat up straight. "Wait…you haven't…you don't…"

Dev had to look away.

She gasped. "Oh. Em. Gee. You *like* him."

"I don't know how it happened! I can't help it! My hands were tied! Not literally—that didn't happen. But it doesn't matter. We're done. It was temporary insanity, and it's over."

"Right." She bit her lip. "Not just because of me, right? I don't want to be an asshole. Am I being an asshole?"

"No! It's because of me. Because we have the biggest competition of our lives starting in two days, and I can't allow any distractions." He certainly needed to stop worrying that Misha could end up in a Siberian gulag if he didn't win. *Only one of us can take the gold.* "And besides, it's ludicrous. We don't even know each other. He's Russian! I'm American!" *And he's moving to America after the Games.* Dev ignored the little voice in his mind. "It didn't mean anything for either of us."

"Okay. One more question. Who came on to who? Or whom, or whatever the hell it's supposed to be."

"In Kyoto it was…mutual. We were in each other's faces and then…"

"You were eating each other's faces."

Dev laughed. "Exactly. Then in the shower the other day it was him. He got on his knees and started blowing me."

Bailey shook her head. "And now you are *blowing my freaking mind.* Up is down. Down is up! And so on. It's definitely never boring with you, Devassy Avira."

"Hey! Only my parents get to call me that." He snapped the towel at her playfully.

"Oh it's on." Bailey grabbed a pillow from the closest bed and walloped him with it.

As Dev retaliated with his pillow, Bailey shrieked in laughter, and Dev had never been so happy to hear it.

IT HAD BEEN difficult to sleep after the incredible high of marching in the opening ceremony with thousands of athletes from around the world. The American team was huge as always, and Dev had met so many new people whose names he'd never keep straight. But now in the frigid morning as he and Bailey piled off the shuttle with the other American pairs and hustled into the arena, the mood was serious. The short program was in a little more than twenty-four hours, and it was time to focus completely.

The previous group still had ten minutes on the ice. The practice order for the groups was switched daily, but Misha's group was once again just before Dev and Bailey's. Dev resolutely kept his eyes off the ice while he and Bailey waited near the Kiss and Cry.

Louise stood off to the side, letting Dev and Bailey be in their heads together as they slapped hands in an elaborate version of patty-cake they'd perfected over the years. Their hands moved in a blur, slapping high and low and back and forth. Whenever one of them needed to calm down, this was their distraction. They both needed it this morning.

They'd just finished their second round when a collective cry of gasps and exclamations filled the arena. Dev looked up as Kisa Kostina flew through the air and across the ice for days before slamming into the boards and bouncing off. One of the other Russian men stumbled to the ice.

Dev's heart pounded as he watched Misha skid to his knees and hover over a crumpled Kisa. Misha turned his head and shouted something in Russian, but the medics were already on the ice, moving slowly in their boots. Kisa was still conscious, and pushed herself onto her knees, clutching her middle. She didn't make a sound, but her face was wrenched with obvious agony.

Beside Dev, Bailey watched with her hands clamped over her mouth. He drew her against him with his arm tightly around her shoulders. Despite what anyone might think, in Dev's experience skaters never wanted to see their competitors get injured. Collisions in particular rattled everyone, and you could hear a pin drop in the arena.

Dev wasn't sure who had been at fault, but the Russian who'd collided with Kisa watched the medics go to work with his hands on his head, shock and dismay clear on his face. He seemed uninjured. Beside him, his partner wept. The Russian federation would *not* be pleased if the gold medal slipped away.

"I don't think she hit her head," Bailey whispered. "That's good."

"She's talking. Maybe she can just shake it off."

Louise hovered behind them. "She was landing a throw and he was skating backward. Their partners tried to warn them, but it was too late."

It didn't seem as though Kisa was going to shake it off. Misha gently scooped her up in his arms and carried her to the nearest exit from the rink, where more paramedics waited with a stretcher. In a few moments they had her strapped on. The crowd clapped for her as the stretcher disappeared into the back of the arena, Misha following close behind with a medic patting his back.

Then there was nothing left to do but go on. The practice session finished with the distraught young Russian team leaving the ice right away. As Dev and Bailey waited to be called to the ice, he thought of Misha's anguished shout and tormented expression. He hugged Bailey tightly, not sure if he was comforting her or himself.

She squeezed him and rubbed his back. "We're okay. Right?" She peered up at him knowingly.

He nodded and kissed her forehead.

Nearby, Caroline blinked away tears while Grant leaned down with his hands on her shoulders, whispering intently. It was clear they were all shaken. Figure skating was seen as so beautiful and elegant, but one wrong move—especially in pairs—and it could end in disaster.

Bailey blew out a long breath and stepped back. "Okay. We got this." She jumped in place, rolling her head, before holding out her fist.

Dev bumped it with his own. "Just another day at the rink."

Bailey nodded. "Just another run-through."

When they took the ice, they circled a few times to warm up and get rid of the jitters. As he stroked around the rink with Bailey's small hand gripping his, Dev couldn't help but worry about Misha. As pair guys, their number-one job was to protect the girls. This was drilled into them from day one. Their partners were extremely vulnerable being spun and flipped and thrown into the air, and it was the man's responsibility to make sure nothing happened to them.

Even though the collision surely hadn't been Misha's fault, Dev knew how he felt watching his partner get loaded into an ambulance. He shivered at the memory. It had happened five years ago one day in practice on a side-by-side spin they'd done a thousand times. For higher marks their spins needed to be closer together, but on this day they'd gotten too close on their camel spins with legs outstretched.

Dev's blade had nicked Bailey's left temple and she'd crashed to the ice in a heap as blood pooled shockingly fast beneath her head. Although it hadn't required surgery and the stitches barely left a scar, the minutes while they waited for the ambulance had been the longest of Dev's life. He and Louise had tried to stop the bleeding, but head injuries gushed.

They weren't sure who had gotten too close to whom, but Dev had felt completely responsible. And although Bailey had been back on the ice in two days, the accident haunted Dev. Bailey, always so fearless, had barely missed a beat, growling and calling herself Frankenstein and walking around with her arms straight out. They'd finally gone to a sports psychologist to work through Dev's guilt and fear, and seeing Misha's stricken expression brought the memories flooding back. But now wasn't the time for it. He had to let it go.

Taking a deep breath, he drew her close and pressed a kiss to her temple.

She squeezed his waist. "Ready?"

"Absolutely."

The rest of the practice went by in a blur. They kept their concentration and had a good run-through of their short. While Bailey returned to the village, Dev slipped on his sneakers and took advantage of the paved sidewalk that ringed the arena. The sun poked through clouds, and he put on his sunglasses and turned up his MP3 player, hoping the latest One Direction remix would carry him away. Bailey had loaded his player with boy bands at Skate Canada in the fall as a joke, but he secretly liked it. Yet today he couldn't shut off his brain.

He wondered how Kisa was doing. How Misha was holding up. The gasp that had filled the arena as Kisa spun into the boards echoed in his mind on a loop.

Dev ran until the twinge in his knee told him it was enough. He'd worked very hard to avoid an injury in the Olympic year, and he wasn't going to ruin it now. That certainly wouldn't help anyone but perhaps the teams nipping at his heels.

He wished he could call Misha and find out what was happening. Text, even. But of course he realized he didn't even have Misha's number. Dev barked out a laugh, his breath a fog in the cold air. They'd had sex more than once, and he didn't even have the man's phone number. *If that's not a snapshot of everything that's wrong with this "relationship," I don't know what is.*

Heading into the dressing room, he passed an uncharacteristically somber Roger Jackman.

Roger shook his head. "Hell, we all want to beat them, but not like this," he murmured.

Dev nodded. "Tell me about it."

"See you tomorrow." Roger clapped Dev's shoulder. "Who the hell knows what'll happen?"

Stomach clenching, Dev walked inside. Misha sat on one of the far benches, his head in his hands. It was all Dev could do not to run to him, but the three Chinese men competing in pairs were sitting near the makeup mirrors, chattering quietly. Still, Dev wanted desperately to pull Misha into his arms, stroke his hair, and tell him everything would be all right. *I barely know him. I need to stay focused. I can't get wrapped up in his problems. Competition starts tomorrow.*

But Dev didn't have it in him to just ignore Misha. If he couldn't hold and kiss him, at least he could talk. Clearing his throat, he took out his earbuds and wrapped them around his slim player. He stood near Misha. "Hey. How's Kisa?"

Misha sat up and rummaged in his bag, not meeting Dev's gaze. "Getting X-rays on her ribs. I came back for our things."

"Couldn't someone else do that?"

"Yes, but I can't just—" He waved his hand. "Stand around in hospital. Better to be busy." He pulled out a T-shirt and began rolling it methodically. "I should have seen him coming."

"It wasn't your fault." Dev knew the words sounded hollow.

"I wish it was me. It should be me." He gave up on the T-shirt and rubbed his face. "Why did this happen? All those years. The work. Poof."

Dev had to physically hold himself back from reaching for him. With another glance at the Chinese skaters, he nodded toward the bathrooms.

After a few moments, Misha followed. In the bathroom Dev quickly checked the stalls—*because I'm in high school for fuck's sake*—and nudged Misha into the farthest one, snapping the lock shut behind them. In the tight space there was barely an inch between them although Dev's back was against the door. But it didn't matter, because Dev couldn't resist pulling Misha into his arms. With a sigh, Misha folded against him like a rag doll, his head on Dev's shoulder.

For a minute they simply stood there, and Dev rubbed Misha's back gently. Then he felt dampness on his neck, and Misha's shoulders quivered.

"Shh. It's all right," Dev whispered. "It's all right."

If someone had told him at the start of the season that at the Olympic Games he'd comfort Mikhail Reznikov while he cried, he would have laughed so hard he might have pissed himself. First off, robots didn't *cry*, and second, they weren't even friendly, let alone friends. Now Dev didn't know what the hell they were, but he couldn't let go as Misha wept, his breath tickling Dev's throat.

When Misha raised his head, his eyes bleary and red rimmed, Dev kissed him tenderly. "It's all right," he repeated.

Then they were truly kissing, and like a flash fire, warm sympathy blazed into hot craving. Hungrily they gripped each other, rutting together, and although the only sounds they made were wet *smacks* of their lips and shuddering breaths, Dev knew the other skaters could come in at any moment and hear them.

Somehow that thought only made the need scorching his veins boil over, and he grabbed Misha's ass, rocking their hips together. It was like the first time in Kyoto, except now there was so much more than lust and anger. Concern and undeniable affection flowed into the mix, and it made Dev's head spin. With Misha he felt exposed and protected at the same time. In danger yet safe. Cold but so, so warm.

Needing to feel flesh on flesh, Dev grappled with their track pants and underwear until he had their cocks tightly in his grasp. Misha whimpered in his ear, and it was a beautiful sound. Dev stroked them both roughly. The friction had him moaning into Misha's mouth as they kissed again, tongues winding together.

Their cocks thrummed against each other, precum slicking the heads, and Dev jacked them harder and faster, their kisses growing ever more desperate. He panted, sweat prickling the back of his neck.

Misha's lips brushed his ear. "I wish you could fuck me right now. I would bend over and take all of you. Every inch. I'd be so good for you as you stretched me open and filled me with your—"

Head smacking against the stall door, Dev spurted over his hand, the pleasure radiating through his body as he bit down on the cry that ripped from his throat, convulsing against Misha again and again, until he was left trembling. With a few more tugs, Misha followed, his mouth open on Dev's neck as he shuddered his release. Misha murmured words Dev couldn't understand against his skin.

When Misha stood tall, flushed, and messy with tears and satisfied lust, his gaze fell to Dev's sticky hand. With a gleam in his eyes, he lifted it to his lips and slowly licked Dev's fingers clean, sucking each one into the heat of his mouth.

Dev's pulse spiked again. "Are you trying to kill me?" he whispered.

Before Misha could answer, a man's voice rang out, speaking Russian. Misha jerked back, dropping Dev's hand as he almost tumbled onto the toilet. Dev gripped his shirt to steady him. Misha's eyes were wide, and he swallowed hard. He called out a reply. The man answered, sounding gruff and angry, but that was generally how most Russians sounded to Dev's ear.

Misha said something else, and they listened to the sound of the man's shoes squeaking on the tile as he walked away. Dev opened his mouth, but Misha jerked his finger to Dev's lips with a violent shake of his head. The seconds ticked by. After a full minute, Misha perched on the toilet and peeked over the top of the stall. Exhaling, he nodded to Dev, and they quickly exited.

At the sink, they both washed their hands. Misha avoided Dev's gaze, his shoulders tense and mouth a thin line. He muttered something to himself in Russian as he shook his head.

In the strained silence, Dev cleared his throat, aware that others could very well now be listening from the adjacent dressing room. "Well, if there's anyone who can come back from this, it's Kisa. She's tough as nails."

"It is impossible." Misha's expression was closed off, and he still didn't meet Dev's gaze.

"Nothing's impossible."

Misha looked up sharply. "She can't breathe without pain like being stabbed. How can she skate?"

"Don't give up yet."

"Why not?" He tore a ream of paper towels from the dispenser. "It was foolish to ever think—" He stopped abruptly.

Dev's heart thumped. "What?" He reached for Misha, but the moment he touched his shoulder, Misha jerked away.

"No. It's over. We can't."

Dev had a sinking feeling the "we" wasn't Misha and Kisa, and his stomach churned. He should be glad. He never should have started this madness in the first place, but now the thought of it ending made him sick.

"We can't...you can't give up without a fight." Dev lowered his voice to a whisper. "Misha, it's okay. We can—"

"No." He balled up the paper towel. "You should want us to give up."

"Why would I want that?" He wasn't sure what they were talking about now.

"Now you can win! Your Bailey is probably happy. *You* should be happy."

Hurt stabbed Dev's gut. "Is that really what you think of me? After..." He clenched his jaw. "We want to *beat* you. Fair and square. Not like this. Bailey would never wish this on anyone. Don't talk about her like that. Or like anything. You don't know her."

Misha scoffed. "We both know very little in skating is fair and square. You will win any way possible. You try to distract me."

"I think you had a little something to do with it," Dev hissed. "Don't act like I was alone in this."

But Misha wouldn't even look at him, his furious gaze locked on the sinks. "And you talk of Kisa. Call her a bitch."

"No, *you* said people think she's a bitch. When I say she's tough as nails, I mean it as a compliment!"

"Bullshit!" Misha kicked the garbage can, sending it crashing onto its side. "You Americans are all the same. You pretend to be friend, but you are liar," he spat.

They stared at each other, nostrils flaring. Dev curled his fingers into fists, anger and confusion warring in him. "You know what? Fuck you. You think you're so much better than us? You're an arrogant asshole, and I wish I'd never met you, let alone—"

"Hello. Guys?"

With a deep breath, Dev looked to the doorway. One of the Chinese skaters hovered there, with a German and Brit behind, all watching with wide eyes.

The Chinese skater spoke again. "It is okay? You are okay?"

Nodding, Dev brushed by them. Fuck this. He was at the biggest competition of his life, and he didn't need this. He didn't need Misha. What Dev needed was to put the drama on the ice—and keep it there.

Chapter Seven

"**T**HEY HAVEN'T WITHDRAWN yet, but no one's seen them," Caroline said, speaking quietly.

"They drew the final flight, so they still have time. But no one knows. It's like this big mystery." Bailey glanced around. They were in one of the long hallways backstage at the arena, and she waited for a Canadian team to walk by before going on. "But I heard one of her ribs is cracked."

"You know the Russian federation is going to milk this for every drop of drama they can," Grant noted with an eye roll.

Dev couldn't disagree. "If there's one thing the Russian federation likes, it's drama." He thought of how they'd kept Misha and Kisa under their thumb, and his stomach churned. What would happen to Misha if they couldn't skate? Would the federation and government blame him? Would he and Kisa be punished?

"Not to mention they like winning," Bailey added. "They'll shoot her up with cortisone or whatever it takes. Not to mention Kisa and Mikhail are fierce. They're not going to give up." She glanced at Dev. "Which I can admire. Begrudgingly, but still."

The music for the pair on the ice ended, and polite applause filled the arena. Dev checked the large clock on the wall. "One more team, and then it's us. We'd better get ready."

They all wore warm-up suits over their costumes, and they stripped them off and returned to their coaches. Dev and Bailey were costumed in simple black with silver accents on the sleeves and necklines, and Bailey had her hair pulled into a tight bun. There was a tiny bump on Dev's chest where he wore his jade elephant, but it wasn't noticeable to anyone who wasn't looking for it.

Louise raised an eyebrow when they approached. "Find out any good gossip?"

"We're curious! We can't help it, Lou." Bailey reapplied her lip gloss.

"I'll only say this one more time. Forget the Russians. Focus on your skate. That's all that matters."

Bailey and Dev nodded, and Dev rolled his shoulders. "We're ready."

The six-minute warm-up went smoothly. The teams were careful to give each other wide berths. Bailey and Dev practiced their jumps twice and nailed them, and Dev concentrated on getting down into his knees and really feeling the ice. If his legs and body were stiff, the program wouldn't flow the way it should.

Relax. Breathe.

They separated for a minute to get in their heads and then came together again, holding hands automatically as they'd done for years. They were first up, so they cut their warm-up short by a minute to go stand by the boards and get last minute instructions from Louise.

"Focus on every movement. Stay in the moment, and don't let it get away from you. You can do this. You're ready. This is your time to shine." Louise smiled. "So shine." She pressed a kiss to each of their cheeks.

Butterflies flapped in Dev's stomach, and he took a last sip of water from a bottle Louise kept for him. As the announcer called time on the warm-up and instructed the other pairs to leave the ice, Dev and Bailey turned away from the boards with a last smile for Louise. They both breathed deeply, standing a foot apart.

The female announcer spoke first in French and then English. "Our next competitors, representing the United States of America—Bailey Robinson and Dev Avira."

As the crowd roared, Dev held up his palm with a flourish. "Let's do this thing."

Bailey took his hand with her own dramatic arm sweep. "We got this."

Wide smiles in place, they glided out with free legs outstretched and acknowledged the crowd. At center ice, they skated around for a few seconds, using their final moments to prepare before taking their starting position. They stood back to back, heads high, expressions serious. For a few moments, there was silence. Dev sucked a breath deep into his lungs.

With a powerful violin chord, they were off.

For two minutes and fifty seconds, they skated together with power and conviction, their program building in intensity with the propulsive music as they ticked off the elements one by one while still making sure there was an electric connection between them. The twist was solid, and their side-by-side toes absolutely bang on. Spins, footwork and the lift, and then the throw. Dev hurled Bailey into the air, and she landed in a perfect glide on a swell in the music. The crowd roared.

They'd done it! *No! Focus! I still have the lift!*

Dev brought himself back, tamping down the excitement and preparing for their final element. Bailey went up over his head, and he turned, his feet smooth and steady. He changed directions, thighs burning as he put in everything he had to keeping up the speed as they went from one end of the rink all the way to the other. He swooped Bailey down for the dismount and they skated into their final pose, back to back just as they had started.

The applause was thunderous, and Dev could swear the ice was vibrating with it. It flowed into him like a shot of adrenaline. He pumped his fist in the air, and Bailey leaped into his arms.

"Yes!" she screamed.

The next few minutes were a blur of waves and hugs and kisses. In the Kiss and Cry they accepted flowers and toys from the little girls who collected them from the ice. Bailey sat between Dev and Louise, who grinned from ear to ear. Pop music played in the arena as they waited for the marks to be tabulated. When the replays finished, Dev waved a stuffed blue elephant at the camera, and he and Bailey blew kisses and called out thanks and love to the people at home. Then the music faded, and Dev's pulse raced. Bailey put her hand on his thigh, her eyes glued to the scoreboard.

"The scores please for Bailey Robinson and Dev Avira of the United States of America," the announcer intoned.

As always, there was a cruelly long pause, and Dev thought his heart might beat right out of his chest.

"The short program score please." Another pause, and the crowd murmured anxiously. "They have earned 81.03 points in the short program. This is a new personal best for Bailey Robinson and Dev Avira."

Dev scanned the breakdown of the scores on the monitor. Technical elements—44.66. Program components—36.37. He raised his arms in the air. "Woo!"

"Bailey Robinson and Dev Avira are currently in first place."

The three of them hugged and celebrated, and Dev's face hurt from smiling. They were ahead of the next team by fifteen points, but there were still some heavy hitters left to come. *And Misha might be one of them.*

As the next team was introduced, Dev and Bailey gathered their flowers and went backstage. Sue, Gabby, and a couple other Feds were waiting. Sue grinned and hugged them both.

"Wonderful job! We're all so proud of you."

Dev kissed her cheek. "Thanks, Sue." The federation and its internal politics could be a pain, but they'd still supported Dev and Bailey over the years.

Gabby beamed. "I'll take you over to the journalists and—"

A growing buzz from one of the hallways made them all turn. With a media scrum surrounding them, cameras flashing and recording, Kisa and Misha walked to the dressing rooms, pulling their little suitcases behind them. All the skaters brought their carry-ons to competition to cart their makeup and costumes and anything they might possibly need. The Russian federation officials and coaches tried to keep the media at bay while Kisa and Misha smiled and kept their gazes forward.

"Well. I guess they're going to try it," Sue noted with clear disappointment.

"They don't have anything to lose," Louise said. "Dev and Bailey nailed it. Let the Russians try and match it."

AS THE CROWD thundered, Dev's heart sank. Guilt followed a moment later.

Bailey stopped in her tracks where she'd been pacing endlessly in the quiet little corner they'd found backstage. They'd both spent time talking and texting with friends and family back home, and now Bailey put her cell in her hoodie pocket and sighed.

"No mistakes."

"Nope."

"I've got to hand it to her. That's impressive. Both of them."

Dev nodded. He hadn't told Bailey that he and Misha had almost come to blows. While he'd promised to always be honest, they had enough drama to deal with. Of course that was why he hadn't told her about Misha in the first place...

"Are you...how do you feel?" Bailey frowned. "About him, I mean."

"I don't know. I change my mind every two minutes." He sighed. "We had a fight yesterday."

"Oh. About what? I mean, aside from the obvious."

Dev didn't see the point in telling her what Misha had said. He smiled grimly. "Just that stuff. He was stressed about the accident, obviously, and it turns out it's a bad idea to sleep with your competition. Makes everything even more complicated. I just feel like…" He ran a hand through his hair.

"What?" she asked quietly.

"It was so much easier when I could just hate them. But now I know all these things, and I worry about what will happen to him." Dev glanced around to make sure they were still alone. "Being gay in Russia can be dangerous. I don't want…I just want him to be okay."

Bailey blinked. "Do you think they'd do something to him?"

"I don't know. I hope not. I hope it's only fear tactics. The Russian government can be pretty scary. They spy on him with these organizations that are basically the KGB with new acronyms."

Her eyes widened. "Shit, seriously?"

Dev nodded miserably. "I'm angry with him and worried about him and I resent him and care about him all at the same time."

"Sounds exhausting, Devassy." She wrapped her arms around him. "It was seriously easier when he was the enemy. We all want to win, and only one team can. We did our job, and it sounds like they did theirs. So it's up to the judges, and we both know how completely fair and always impartial the judges are."

Hugging her back, Dev snorted. "Completely. But one thing I do know for sure is that I'm damn proud of us."

Bailey pulled back. "You and me both." As the audience hooted and hollered for what had to be the end of Kisa and Misha's program, she linked her arm through his. "Come on, let's go hear the scores."

They joined the group of people by the monitors backstage,

including Louise, Sue, and Gabby, and the other US teams. Kisa grimaced as she stepped off the ice, and their coach crouched down to put on her skate guards for her. Misha gently helped her sit at the Kiss and Cry.

Grant whistled. "Whoa. She's in serious pain."

The slo-mo replays began, showing the perfect side-by-side Salchows and the giant split triple twist.

"Man, you wouldn't know it the way they skated," Caroline said. "Amazing." She flushed and looked at Dev and Bailey. "Sorry, guys."

"It's the truth," Bailey replied. She smiled. "Don't be sorry, Sweet."

The latest Lady Gaga song cut out and the announcer came on the loudspeaker. "The scores please for Kisa Kostina and Mikhail Reznikov of Russia." An interminable pause. "The short program score please." *Another* interminable pause. "They have earned 83.01 points. This is a new season's best for Kisa Kostina and Mikhail Reznikov."

"Not even their personal best and they still beat us. With a broken rib," Bailey muttered. She sighed and then put on a smile for the cameras.

"Kisa Kostina and Mikhail Reznikov are currently in first place."

"It's less than two points. That's nothing. She held up through the short, but four and a half minutes will be another matter," Louise said, in a tone that brooked no argument. "You're in the perfect position."

Dev couldn't help but think that first place was the perfect position, but he nodded. Kisa and Misha went by with their coaches, Kisa still in obvious pain, Misha supporting her gently. He was sweaty and beautiful and Dev's heart clenched despite himself. Maybe he and Misha should talk and—

No! Enough!

Not Misha. He was *Mikhail,* Dev's rival. Dev couldn't think about what would happen to Mikhail if he didn't win. It wasn't Dev's problem. It *couldn't* be. Dev and Bailey were *thisclose* to realizing their lifelong dream, and he couldn't give up now.

Chapter Eight

THE TENSION IN the dressing room the next night was so thick Dev felt as though he was swimming in it. Or more accurately drowning in it. His heart rate was all over the place and he needed to *breathe*. But it was easier said than done when the four men in the room who would be skating in the final flight were all aiming for the podium. For the gold.

Of course add in the completely fucked-up *whatever* that was happening between Dev and Misha—*no*. Mikhail. It was enough to make him want to tear off his costume and run. Possibly screaming and waving his arms.

Roger, usually so talkative, gave Dev a stiff smile before leaving. He and his partner were in third place and four points back of Dev and Bailey. The rest of the teams down to sixth were separated by less than two points. Anything could happen. Dev's stomach churned. They still had to deliver. There was no guarantee they'd stay on the podium, let alone win. They had to be perfect.

Leading up to an event, Dev knew exactly what and when to eat, how to practice, and how much sleep to get. Before the short program he'd allowed himself to be distracted, but in the last day everything else had fallen away and he'd zeroed in on preparing for the long program. This was the most important night of his life, and nothing else could interfere.

Admittedly it had helped that with the shuffling of group order for practices, he hadn't seen Mikhail until now. Dev tucked his elephant charm under his navy shirt and adjusted his white cravat. Without a glance at any of the remaining skaters, he walked to the door. As he left, he thought he could feel a searing gaze on his back, but it was surely his imagination.

In the backstage area, Bailey was resplendent in her high-necked navy dress. Along with the white trim, it was subtly shot through with silver thread that caught the light and matched her gleaming earrings, simple Celtic knots. It was often said that in pairs skating, the man was the stem and the woman the flower, or he the frame and she the picture. In every movement, Dev aimed to display Bailey at her most beautiful and elegant, and she certainly made his job easy. He kissed her cheek.

While Louise stood a few feet away, giving them their space to prepare, Bailey jumped up and down a few times and then raised her hands for patty-cake. They whipped through their pattern at record speed, repeating it four times before Bailey stepped into his arms. No words were necessary, and he held her tightly.

By the time they took the ice for their performance, Dev was strangely calm. At the Olympics the long program was skated in reverse order of the standings from the short, putting them second to last. Only two teams in the top ten had made mistakes, and the arena hummed with the positive energy that clean skates created. They just needed to ride that wave. Of course on the flipside, even one mistake could knock them off the podium.

The first time their choreographer played the *Jane Eyre* score for them, Dev and Bailey had fallen in love with it immediately. Although lyrics were permitted in all the skating disciplines now, they both agreed they wanted to go traditional. The fact that somehow it had never been skated to sealed the deal. In any given season there were multiple Carmens, Phantoms, Swan Lakes, and Sleeping Beauties across the disciplines, and while their short program music had been used in the past, they wanted something for the long that was solely theirs. It was their signature program.

As the cheers from the crowd faded, he placed his hand on Bailey's shoulder for their starting position. Standing behind her, he was the imposing Mr. Rochester to her young governess Jane. Bailey kept her gaze on the ice.

This is it. This is my moment. I just have to take it.

The music began, and in unison, Dev's hand still on Bailey's shoulder, they pushed off into a simple glide with free legs extended. Recorded by a small orchestra with hardly any brass or percussion, the score highlighted piano and especially violin solos. Their selection began sweet and forlorn as they moved into a spiral step sequence. Moving with the music, letting it flow through him in every pore, Dev performed the steps they'd practiced over and over again since the summer.

They gathered speed for their triple toe/double toe combinations, and the crowd exploded when they landed in perfect unison. Adrenaline pumping through him, Dev breathed as they set up for the twist. He caught Bailey above his shoulders and set her down smoothly.

They skated with speed and grace, and when the slow section at the midpoint began, Dev caressed Bailey's cheek and she gazed at him with wide, beseeching eyes. They were Rochester and Jane, torn apart by deception. They caught their breath with a back-outside death spiral, Bailey's free leg in the air and back arched exquisitely. They moved into their side-by-side spins as a plaintive violin solo filled the arena.

We're doing it. We're doing it! Focus, focus, focus.

When the tempo and power of the music built again, Dev put his hands on Bailey's waist and they prepared for their first throw. It was past the halfway point of their program when all jumps, throws and lifts received a 10 percent bonus in the marks. He launched her into the air, and she spun tightly, muscling out the landing and having to touch her free leg down to keep her balance. It was a small mistake, and there was no time to think of it because they were headed into their triple Salchows.

Bam! Nailed them.

Heart pumping, Dev hoisted Bailey up smoothly, his arms burning but making it look as if she weighed nothing at all in the first of their three lifts, all in the last half to maximize points. He reversed the rotation halfway through the lift for extra points, keeping the momentum going with every fiber of his being.

Violins soared for the second throw, and this time Bailey landed perfectly with a smile splitting her face, arms to the heavens. Into their next lift, they were Rochester and Jane—reunited! The violins were joyful, the score swelling as they flew into their pairs combination spin, contorting themselves around each other in various positions as they spun.

One more element. Go, go, go!

With the crowd already cheering, Dev could barely hear the music as he and Bailey both skated into their last lift, a backward lasso. Dev lifted her above his head and they moved to a one-handed position, Bailey gripping Dev's hand at her belly as she reached behind with her other hand to hook her skate blade and lift her foot high. Dev's legs screamed, the lactic acid searing his muscles as he pushed himself to his limit.

He set Bailey down with one hand, and they stroked with back crossovers around the corner of the rink as the violins crescendoed. Dev slid to his knee and lifted his arms to Bailey, pressing his face to her breasts as he hugged her desperately. She gazed to the heavens on the last beat of the music, one leg extended behind her on the ice.

The audience erupted, and Dev gasped for breath, clinging to Bailey.

We did it.

Bailey leaned over him, hugging him as she panted, her chest heaving. "Oh my God. Oh my God," she muttered.

"We did it, B." Dev pushed to his feet and swung her around.

The crowd was on its feet, whistling and screaming, and as Dev and Bailey skated to center ice for their bows, Dev had to blink back tears. They bowed to each side of the arena, smiling and waving. Dev knew he should be exhausted, but it was as if he were skating on air as they made their way to the Kiss and Cry.

Louise pumped her fist. "That's how it's done." She tackled them in hugs before they could even put on their guards and get off the ice.

The crowd was still cheering, and Dev could barely sit down, instead perching on the edge of the bench in the Kiss and Cry as the flowers and toys began arriving. He shouted to his family and friends, and he and Bailey hugged and kissed again, Bailey slapping his knee.

"Oh my God," she repeated, wiping the sweat from her brow.

The wait for the scores was even more torturous, and the crowd began clapping in rhythm, the whole arena echoing with it as they waited for the announcer's voice.

"The scores please for Bailey Robinson and Dev Avira of the United States of America."

Dev's breath lodged in his throat, and Bailey's fingers dug into his thigh.

"The free skate score please."

Yes, yes—GIVE US THE FUCKING SCORE!

"They have earned 158.76 points in the free skate. This is a new personal best for Bailey Robinson and Dev Avira."

Dev and Bailey leaped to their feet in unison, arms thrust high, screaming their joy. Dev shouted, "Yes! Yes!" They hugged again, spinning and laughing and yanking a beaming Louise up to join them.

"Bailey Robinson and Dev Avira are currently in first place."

They'd beaten the Canadians, and a silver medal was guaranteed. But it could still be gold. The only team that could beat them were on the ice, waiting for the pandemonium to die down. Dev watched as Mikhail and Kisa stood ramrod straight, shoulders down, heads high as they waited by the boards for their names to be called.

For a moment, he thought of the freedom this gold medal represented for Misha, and the urge to wish him luck swelled in Dev's chest.

"Jesus, I can't watch. Let's go hide," Bailey said as they picked up their gifts and went beyond the curtain.

But there would be no hiding as the federation well-wishers swept them up into hugs and chatter and other skaters congratulated them—some more genuinely than others. Dev's heart thumped as *Firebird* filled the arena.

As Stravinsky's music began, a wave of feeling seemed to wash from the audience to the people backstage. The chatter died and all eyes turned to the monitors. Standing behind Bailey, Dev held on to her shoulders, grounding them both. He could feel the tension in her body that matched his own as the triple twist exploded high into the air. It was the best in the world, there was no question.

As Mikhail and Kisa went into their triple-double combinations, Dev was very aware of the TV crew filming them as they watched, and he kept his expression neutral. As they landed perfectly, Dev was torn between disappointment and pride. God, he wanted to win so badly, but what Mikhail and Kisa were doing was remarkable.

The feeling grew as the flawless performance continued. Maybe it was the pain and upset of the collision and injury, but to Dev's eyes, Misha—*Mikhail, Mikhail, Mikhail*—and Kisa were finally skating with a passion and true connection to match their technical brilliance. While the judges had always overscored them on their program components, for the first time Dev really felt as though they were earning them.

Their last element was a throw in the final moments of their program—a huge risk that could pay dividends if Kisa landed it, and mar the program completely if she missed. This one jump would make the difference. As she spun into the air, so high her feet were above the boards, Dev could feel the thousands of people in the arena holding their breath as one.

On a beautiful edge with a deep knee bend, Kisa glided into her landing. The crowd erupted.

All Dev could do was squeeze Bailey's shoulders and watch. After hitting the final pose, Kisa doubled over in obvious agony, her hands on her knees. As Misha leaned down and kissed her head with tears in his eyes, Dev's heart clenched. Through his haze of disappointment, a wave of affection for Misha and admiration for Kisa washed over him. Their performance would go down in the history books.

With a smile in place, Bailey tugged Dev's hand. "Let's go get ready for the ceremony," she said loudly in a decidedly perky tone.

They waved to the cameras and gave thumbs-up to all the folks at home as they escaped down the hallway to the dressing rooms. They didn't need to hear the scores. They'd done their best, but it wasn't enough. As reality set in, Dev flip-flopped between numb acceptance and bitter disappointment.

In a far dark corner out of sight of the cameras, Bailey blinked back tears. "It's not fair. It's not fucking fair. We had it, Dev. We had it! Just once, why couldn't we be better? We worked so hard." She shook her head. "God damn it. They were perfect." Her shoulders slumped. "They really were. I don't know how she did it. And maybe tomorrow I'll think it was amazing. But tonight it hurts so much to come so close."

"We did everything we could. We did our best, Bailey."

Her lip trembled. "I put my foot down on that throw."

"Shh." Dev held her close. "That was one point. Forget it."

"That might have been the difference, Dev! I mean, I know it wasn't. I know they're going to put up a new world record for that. But I still wanted to be perfect. God, I just want to go home and cry." She breathed deeply and pulled back. "But I can't, because we've got to go get our silver medal and smile and pretend we're not dying inside." She tried to smile and failed miserably, her eyes glistening. "And maybe tomorrow the silver won't seem so bad. But tonight it feels like someone carved out my insides with a rusty spoon."

Dev nodded miserably. "But I'm proud of you. Proud of us. We did our best ever. It was pretty damn close to perfect. Gordeeva and Grinkov had four little mistakes when they won gold again in '94, and that was one of the greatest long programs ever. You know how hard perfect is in this sport."

"Exactly," Louise said, appearing behind them.

"God!" Bailey put her hand to her chest. "Don't do that!"

But it broke the tension, and they all laughed a little. Dev asked, "What was the final score?"

"They won by less than four points. That's the closest it's ever been between you guys. You should be proud. I know it doesn't feel like it right now, but this is a victory."

"See?" Dev raised an eyebrow at Bailey. "The throw didn't matter. They would have beaten us anyway."

Bailey took a tissue from Louise and blew her nose loudly. "Okay."

"Celebrate all the things you did right. I know it's hard, but you set a personal best at the Olympic Games."

"We couldn't have done it without you, Lou. Thank you," Dev said, swallowing thickly.

Bailey nodded vigorously and drew them both into another hug. "I love you both." She pulled back and swiped at her eyes. "Okay, enough mushy stuff because my mascara is going to run all over the place!"

"Go fix it up. You've got time. Kisa's with the medics. That was a real Keri Strug moment at the end. The media's having a masturbatory field day about her grit and determination. I'd roll my eyes, but she earned the hell out of it." She clapped their shoulders. "All right, game faces on. This will feel like the longest medal ceremony of your lives, but remember that very few skaters ever get to stand on an Olympic podium. Hold your heads high and try to enjoy it, even a little bit."

They played their roles as required, as skaters always did. Aside from that one time—but Dev wasn't about to take off his silver medal in protest on the podium and make an ass of himself. Especially since he'd been beaten fair and square. The ceremony was almost like an out-of-body experience, with the only real, electric moment coming when he approached the podium to congratulate the winners.

In that instant Dev knew without a doubt that the man in front of him would never be *Mikhail* again. As their eyes met, Dev felt a surge of emotions he couldn't begin to parse, from a trace of bitterness to pride to lust to a devastating sense of longing that weakened his knees. Mikhail had been the man he'd gone to war against.

Now Misha was the man he was falling in love with.

He took Misha's hand, shivering at the flare of heat that shot through his body. He wanted to say a thousand things. He wanted to talk all night. He wanted to talk for days. Instead he merely nodded. "Congratulations."

Misha held his hand longer than he should have, his gaze intense. "Thank you."

Dev let go and climbed onto the second tier of the podium with his greatest desires inches away but beyond his grasp.

Chapter Nine

"Here's what we're going to do."

Dev blinked and groaned. "Didn't we lock that door?"

"No, actually, you didn't," Bailey said as she breezed inside and stood by Dev's bed with hands on hips.

Andrew burrowed under his duvet. "Again, I could have been naked," he muttered. "Maybe you *want* to see me naked."

"I'm not going to dignify that with a response. Okay, here's the situation, D. For the past three days, we've been moping around and eating our feelings and crying all our tears. Time to make that glass half-full. And not with booze. No, we didn't win gold. But an Olympic silver medal is pretty fantastic. I admit I'm not sure I really feel that yet." She pressed her chest. "You know, in my soul? But I figure if we say it a lot, it'll become like muscle memory and we'll start to believe it." She yanked off Dev's duvet.

"Can't I wallow in another hour of sleep?" Dev knew he was whining but couldn't help it. He reached for the covers, shivering in his boxer briefs.

"The time for wallowing is through. We're going for a run to get those endorphins flowing. No sausage and egg McMuffin again for breakfast this morning. Even though I really, really want one. No. It's back to bran and eggs, my friend. We need to get our shit together. We got beaten, and it sucks. But that's the way this sport goes. That's the way every sport goes. They were better. They rocked it, and Kisa Kostina is going to inspire a new generation of girls to be fierce. If we had to get beaten, I'm glad it was in style."

Dev sighed, thoughts of Misha swirling in his mind accompanied by a dull ache that his tenth-grade English teacher would have called yearning. "I know. You're right."

"Well *duh*. That goes without saying. Come on. The clock is ticking for Worlds, and we have one more chance to stand on the top of that podium. We got this."

"You can do it!" Andrew seemed wide awake now, and he sprang from bed. "You're going to win in Boston, and I'm going to kick ass. I blew my quad toe *and* my Axel in the long yesterday, but I'm going to nail them at Worlds. I may not be near the podium yet, but I'm going to do the US proud. Come on, let's all go for a run." He dashed to the bathroom and paused by the door. "And hey, Bailey, I scored tickets for slopestyle this afternoon. You want to come?"

"I have no idea what that is, but hell yeah. It sounds awesome." She smiled. "Thanks, Andrew."

He flushed. "It's this new skiing thing. Sounds really cool, and…yeah. Okay. Cool. It's a date." He disappeared into the bathroom.

Bailey's brow furrowed. "Wait, what just happened?"

Dev grinned. "I believe you have a social engagement with young Mr. Quinn."

"I guess I do." She shrugged. "What the hell. Speaking of social engagements, we're staying in a veritable hotbed of sexy men, and it's high time we did something about that." She perched on the side of Dev's bed and smiled sadly. "Because I think you're wallowing over more than just the silver."

He couldn't deny it. "I wish I could just put him out of my head."

"Have you talked to him?" she asked quietly.

"You *want* me to talk to him?"

"Look, he's historically not been my favorite person, but in all the years I've known you I've never seen a guy get under your skin like this. He's obviously not *all* bad. He's actually probably pretty wonderful if you like him. And for the record he'd better be wonderful, because if he hurts you, I'll make those Russian spies look like the Golden Girls."

"Been watching reruns, huh?"

"Blanche Devereaux is my spirit guide even when she's dubbed in French." Bailey squeezed Dev's leg. "Kisa and Misha are gliding into the sunset. They already said at last year's Worlds that it would be their last. What's done is done. I'm not going to hold a grudge."

"You're being awfully zen."

"Do you enjoy it? I thought it was worth a shot. So far, so good. But seriously, they're not our competition anymore. He's free game. But please don't start fucking Roger Jackman, because we don't need Worlds to be a dramarama too."

He thumped her with a pillow. "As *if* I'd hook up with Roger. For starters there's no way he's gay. And I think his wife might object."

She giggled and hit him back. "Hey, I never thought Robot Reznikov was gay either."

"He's not a robot."

Bailey smirked. "It's kind of cute when you defend him."

Dev thought of what Misha had said about Bailey and guilt soured his stomach. He shouldn't miss someone who would think that about his best friend. But the hollow in his chest still ached. He sighed. "I'm a fool, Bailey. From the start he said I was just his 'little rebellion.' But I went and fell for him anyway. God, I'm moping around and he probably hasn't given me another thought. He won the gold and he's moving to California, and he doesn't need to rebel anymore. He doesn't need me."

"Then he's a moron and he doesn't deserve you."

Dev fought the urge to defend Misha again. "You know what? Forget him. You're right. Let's go for a run. Put the past in the past and look toward the future."

Bailey shot to her feet with her arm raised and index finger pointed. "Onward and upward. Faster, higher, stronger. Now put on some pants and get your fine ass out of bed."

THE COMMANDING KNOCK echoed through the small room, and Dev slung his towel around his hips, hurrying from the steamy bathroom. "Since when do you knock?" he called. "Andrew went to your room to pick you up." But when he opened the door, it wasn't Bailey standing there.

Head held as regally as ever, Misha stood there, his back ramrod straight. He opened his mouth but then closed it again.

Dev swallowed hard. "Oh. Um, hey. I..." He stepped back. "Come in."

With a small nod, Misha swept by him and stood by the guest chairs. He wore dark jeans and a form-fitting black sweater that showed off his lean muscles and narrow hips. His hair swept over his forehead, and there was a few days' worth of stubble on his face. He was beautiful, as always.

The longing was like the throbbing in Dev's muscles after a long program. He cleared his throat. "I didn't think I'd see you again." He waved his hand. "I mean, obviously I'll see you at the gala performance next week. But I didn't think I'd see you...like this."

"I wasn't sure you wanted to. I thought not."

"But here you are." Dev's pulse thrummed.

"If I'm not welcome, I will leave." Misha took a step toward the door.

"No, no. Stay." The silence stretched out between them, and Dev cast about for something to say. "How's Kisa?"

Misha's lips quirked into a little smile. "Uncomfortable. She is pained whether sitting or lying, and standing is no better. But she rests and has much chocolate and vodka and what's the word? Romance novels that are…ah! Trashy."

Dev laughed. "That's good. She deserves a break. Man, she gritted it out. I admire her." He realized as he said it that it wasn't simply lip service. "She's going to be able to skate in the gala?"

"Nothing could stop her," Misha replied fondly.

"I really do admire her. Both of you. It was an amazing skate. One for the history books."

"Spasibo. You also skated beautifully. You and Bailey." Misha frowned and stood up straighter, clasping his hands behind his back. "I must make an apology. I should not have said those things about Bailey. I knew when I spoke it was untrue. She is an honorable competitor. An honorable woman. Please forgive me."

Warmth bloomed in Dev's chest. "It's okay. You were stressed. We both were."

"It was not okay. You are also an honorable man, and I should not have said otherwise. In that moment, after Vladimir from the federation nearly discovered us…I was very afraid. I acted as if you were the one to blame for my recklessness. As if you were the one to blame for Kisa's injury. It was very unfair. I am ashamed."

Dev wanted to reach for him but crossed his arms awkwardly over his chest instead. *Maybe he's only here to apologize. Maybe that's all he wants.* The few feet between them felt like the Grand Canyon. "Apology accepted. I shouldn't have said what I did either."

Misha stared intently. "Do you still wish those things? That we had never met? That we had never…"

Dev didn't have to think about his answer. "No. Not even a

little bit." He took a deep breath as his heart thumped faster. "Because this thing with you, it's been…" He motioned with his hands, trying to find the words. "Different than anything I've ever experienced. Better than anything I've ever felt. What about you? Does it feel different?"

Misha stepped closer, his eyes bright and breath shaky. "Yes. I cannot explain why. It is not only touching you, but speaking. I want…I want so much. *Vse.* Everything. Everything of you."

Joy and laughter rushed through Dev as he threw his arms around Misha. "Yes. *Everything.*" He breathed in Misha's woodsy cologne and kissed his neck, content to just be in Misha's arms again. Misha held him tightly, his firm body pressing against him.

When they stumbled to Dev's bed—Misha's clothes scattered on the floor along with Dev's towel—Misha straddled Dev's hips and ran his hands over Dev's chest before bending to tease his nipples with fingers and a clever tongue. Misha's new stubble scraped the sensitive flesh, and Dev shivered as his cock swelled.

"Misha," he murmured.

Misha glanced up with lust-darkened eyes. "Oh yes. Say it again."

Dev repeated it as he yanked Misha's head close for a kiss. "I want…" Dev thrust his hips up, moaning.

"Tell me."

Dev had never been one for talking much during sex, but the words spilled out. "I want to fuck you every way I can. I want your ass and your mouth and your cock. I want to come all over you. I want you to come all over me."

Misha muttered something in Russian and reached over the side of the bed to snag his jeans. He pulled a condom and lube packet from his pocket.

Laughing, Dev ran his hands over Misha's strong thighs. "Aren't you the Boy Scout."

A furrow appeared between Misha's brows. "I do not understand." He squeezed the lube onto his fingers and reached back for his hole.

"It means... Never mind. Later. I'll explain..." Dev trailed off as he watched Misha finger himself open with little moans, eyes fluttering shut and a flush rising up his chest. Dev's cock curved to his stomach, hard and straining.

With a sly smile, Misha rolled the condom over Dev and raised up on his knees to sink down. Inch by inch, Dev was engulfed by his heat. He wanted to grip Misha and ram into him, but he grabbed the sheets and let Misha set the pace. "Fuck you're beautiful," Dev whispered. He traced Misha's tattoo with his fingertips.

Head thrown back, his Adam's apple bobbing, Misha rode him. With the same grace and ease he'd always shown on the ice, he rolled his hips, squeezing around Dev's cock. "*Mne tak khorosho.*"

"I have no idea what you're saying, but keep talking."

With a hearty laugh, Misha met Dev's gaze and leaned his hands on Dev's shoulders, changing the angle and groaning. "I say that you feel so good." He licked the hollow of Dev's throat. "You are so good inside me, Dev."

Bending his legs, Dev used the leverage to thrust harder, not able to resist.

"*Da! Vot tak.*" Misha kissed him and murmured, "Like that."

The way Misha slipped into Russian during sex made Dev's balls tighten and sparks tingle on his skin. Digging his heels into the mattress, he found a rhythm and rocked into Misha as Misha slammed down, his cries on every stroke undoubtedly heard all the way in the dining hall. Dev grinned. Let them hear.

Fingers digging into Dev's shoulders, Misha panted and rode desperately, a bead of sweat slipping down his chest, and his hair in his eyes. When he stroked himself roughly he came with a groan and striped Dev's chest, eyes locked with Dev's as he milked himself. He squeezed with his ass, and Dev jerked and shouted, his orgasm sending the sweet burn of pleasure into every pore.

They both breathed deeply, nostrils flaring, and Misha rubbed his hand over Dev's sticky chest, teasing the sparse hair that grew there. "Next you will come on me, yes?"

"Yes, but give me a minute."

A female voice called through the wall. "I need a minute too."

Laughing, Dev covered his face. "Oh my God I hope that's not someone I know," he whispered.

Misha called back, "Next show in twenty minutes!" To Dev he added with a shrug, "This is Athletes' Village. It is a fuckfest." He removed the condom from Dev's cock and tied a knot before merrily tossing it into a garbage can near the door.

Dev laughed again. "We'd better do our part then."

Still straddling Dev's hips, Misha reached to brush his thumb over Dev's bottom lip. "We will go into the mountains also. There is a restaurant there. Very private, they say. With view of the Alps all around and sky so close you can touch." A hopeful smile brightened his face. "If you would like?"

In that moment, the bitter pill of the past few days dissolved into a sense of peace and optimism. Dev smiled back. "I'd like. Very much."

They kissed tenderly. Dev didn't win Olympic gold, but with Misha warm in his arms, he felt as though he'd gained something far more valuable.

Chapter Ten

March: The World Championships

"IN FIRST PLACE, and the winners of the gold medal, representing the United States of America—Bailey Robinson and Dev Avira!"

The home crowd cheered so loudly Dev was certain the arena would fall down around their ears, which would be a shame since he was experiencing one of the greatest moments of his life. His face hurt from grinning, but he couldn't stop as he and a glowing Bailey took their bows and climbed to the top of the podium.

He knew it was silly, but Dev felt as if the air they were breathing from their perch was somehow different. *Better.* The gold disc around his neck was a solid and satisfying weight, and he wondered if it would be completely lame to sleep with it on.

When the anthem began and the flags were raised with the Stars and Stripes in the middle position, Dev and Bailey giddily belted out the words along with just about everyone in the building. Winning Worlds with so many of their family and friends in attendance was more magical than he'd dared hope.

Hands over their soaring hearts, he and Bailey sang. He squeezed her shoulder with his free hand and she reached up to tangle their fingers. For once an awards ceremony was over all too soon, and the audience thundered. Posing for pictures this time was a pleasure, and when they did their victory lap it took almost twenty minutes with all the people they needed to stop and hug. Some were family and some loyal fans, including Amaya and Reiko.

Once Dev and Bailey finally made it around the rink, they were ushered back to the podium, where the network had set up directors' chairs on the carpet for an interview. The TV lights glared on, almost blinding them.

The female reporter gushed. "You were the odds-on favorites here to win a world title after your electrifying performances at the Olympic Games, and you did not disappoint! Neither of you put a foot wrong in this competition. How did it feel to skate a perfect program tonight?"

"It felt like a long time coming," Bailey replied with a chuckle. "After the Olympics we really worked hard to continue improving so we could end our amateur careers as champions. We couldn't be happier."

"And to do it here in your hometown, Dev!" the reporter exclaimed. "This crowd was a hundred percent behind you guys, and it must mean a lot to be able to become world champs with your families here to support you."

"It means everything," Dev said. "Our families have been there through it all with us, and we share these gold medals with them."

"Dev, I know your mother told me she's planning a heck of a party tomorrow night!"

He laughed. "It's true—my mother doesn't do anything in half measures."

"I'm going to eat my weight in masala dosa, just for the record," Bailey noted.

The reporter laughed. "So what are your plans now that your amateur career is over?"

"We'll be touring this summer across North America and Asia, and after that I'm going to check out some colleges and take a few classes," Bailey answered.

"What about you, Dev?"

"I'm not sure. I've thought about getting into coaching, so I'm going to explore my options. Bailey and I both want to continue skating together as professionals as long as we can when opportunities arise, so we won't be taking on anything full-time for a few years yet."

"What about in the next little while? How will you celebrate? Are you going to Disneyland?" The reporter asked with a wink.

Dev found himself smiling. "Actually, I am heading to California for a few weeks before the first tour begins. I think I've earned a vacation."

Bailey gave Dev's knee a squeeze. "He's definitely earned this one."

After a few more questions they were finished, and they made their way to the exit by the Kiss and Cry. Dev stopped and looked to Bailey. "This is it. Our last time on competition ice."

She took a deep breath. "End of an era, D. I wouldn't have wanted to do it with anyone else."

"Me either. Ready, B?"

Eyes shining, she smiled and took his hand. "We got this."

"*ZOLOTO!* COME HERE, silly girl," Misha called to the French bulldog puppy, who barked at the waves as they rolled in.

They had the beach almost to themselves as the sun sank toward the horizon and the lights of the Santa Monica Pier twinkled on. With their jeans rolled above their ankles, Dev and Misha strolled along and threw sticks for the puppy. Dev loved the grit of the sand between his toes.

A salty breeze blew off the water, and Dev zipped his hoodie. "It's getting cold. And don't even say it."

Misha scooped a rock from the sand and skipped it into the

water. "What? I said nothing."

"Uh-huh. But you were thinking it."

Misha still wore just a white T-shirt. "You Americans are so thin-blooded," he teased. "You don't know what cold really is."

"I'm from Boston. It gets cold there, trust me. Plus I lived in Colorado Springs the past six years. Cold!" He bumped Misha's shoulder good-naturedly.

"Zoloto! Come on." Misha tossed a stick across the sand, and she raced after it, tripping over her paws in her frenzy.

"I still haven't decided if naming your dog Gold is charming or arrogant. And a follow-up—I can't believe they're letting you bring her on tour."

He grabbed the stick from the puppy's jaws and tossed it again. "They want Kisa and I to skate in their shows? Zoloto comes as well." He grinned. "I was going to ask for Zoloto to have private dressing room, just to see if they'd agree."

Dev laughed. "Look, you might be an Olympic champion, but you're not JLo. Your ass is too small for starters."

Misha gave him a sly glance. "You have complaint about my ass?"

Dev gave him a pat. "Not even a little bit." At the thought of all the sex they'd had since he arrived in California three weeks ago, heat surged through him, followed by the sinking feeling in his stomach he felt when he remembered it was all ending in a few days.

"What?" Stopping, Misha caressed Dev's cheek with the back of his knuckles. "Thinking of my ass should not make you look so sad."

Dev smiled briefly. "No, it wasn't that." *Might as well just spit it out already.* "I probably shouldn't bring this up and ruin everything, but…" He sighed. "It's been amazing here together, but in a few days we're both leaving. Stars on Ice is starting in Lake Placid, and you and Kisa are going to Europe. Then we'll both be on tour in Asia, which will be awesome, but when the summer ends…then what?"

"There are rinks here in LA. Top coaches you could work with. Be an assistant to start. I spoke to a few people. They are interested."

Dev's heart skipped a beat. "You talked to them about me?"

"I only mentioned you might be back here in the fall. They were very interested. You would be an excellent coach, Dev."

His pulse sped up. "You want me to come back here with you?"

Misha didn't hesitate. "I do. If you like." He caught Dev's hand. "I would like it very much. I know it is quick, but you bring me such delight. We could find a little house together."

"Right on the beach?" Dev smiled. Currently Misha was renting a condo steps from the sand.

"Where else?"

"And what will you do?"

Misha shook his head. "I don't know." He grinned mischievously. "This is Los Angeles. Perhaps I will become a movie star."

"You have the looks."

He kissed Dev softly. "Spasibo." The puppy raced around them, and Misha laughed. "Be calm, Zoloto." His smile faded. "Do you want to know the truth?"

Dev wasn't sure he did. He braced himself. "Okay."

"When we won in Annecy, I had great pride, of course. Happiness, yes, but more…relief. Such relief. It was finally over, and I'd succeeded. The burden is lifted. To me the gold is not the medal." He waved his arm around them. "It's here. The beach in California. Freedom." He chuckled at Zoloto as she wriggled in the sand. "A puppy to spoil." He cupped Dev's cheek. "You. These things are gold."

Dev could hardly breathe. "Misha, I…"

"Say yes."

"Being with you it's…" Dev tried to find the right words.

Misha dropped his hand and stepped back, his gaze going to the sand. "It's all right. Too rushed. I understand."

"Being with you is like a dream I never knew I had."

Misha's head snapped up, his eyes hopeful. "Da?"

"I've spent so many years on one dream. I never thought… I never saw this one coming. But I love being with you. Being here with you. I think we can make it work."

"Yes?" Misha whispered.

He leaned their foreheads together and wrapped his arms around Misha's waist. "Yes. Yes, yes, yes."

With a whoop, Misha bent his knees and lifted Dev off the sand. They spun around before landing in a heap. As they kissed, Dev saw movement from the corner of his eye and pulled away. "She's in the water!"

Misha bolted up and raced into the powerful surf to scoop her up. Dev got to his feet and brushed the sand from his clothes. "Is she okay?"

"I think so." Addressing the soaked puppy in his arms, Misha scolded, "The waves are too strong for little dogs. Silly girl." He was almost soaked himself, and he shivered.

Dev couldn't help a smirk. "What's the matter? A little cold?"

Misha huffed. "Maybe a tiny bit."

"Come on, we should get you out of those clothes." Dev turned back the way they'd come.

"Perhaps you can be of assistance."

"Perhaps." Dev grinned and took off running. "Race you!"

Shouting a Russian curse, Misha bolted after him and soon they sprinted side by side, Zoloto nipping at their heels. Laughter carrying on the wind, they flew toward home.

PART TWO

Chapter Eleven

"**H**OW NICE OF you to join us!"

As Misha pivoted in a crouch, spinning Kisa around in a death spiral, he craned his neck, trying to glimpse the rink entrance. The voice of the tour choreographer, Alice Jenkins, rang out again.

"You Americans, always fashionably late."

Misha spotted a flash of Dev's bright smile as he gave Alice a hug, and his breath caught. A moment later he was sitting on the ice with Kisa sprawled in front of him. With a curse, he quickly hauled her to her feet.

Heart thumping, he watched Dev at the other end of the rink, laughing and greeting the other skaters. Misha fought the urge to race down the ice and swing Dev off his feet. He longed to kiss and touch and breathe him into his lungs again.

With his dark skin and eyes and glossy black hair, Dev was stunning. But it was his smile—one that lit up his entire being—that had secretly drawn Misha to him for years. His joy in skating that had shone from him each time he took the ice. For so long Misha had yearned to touch him. Now to see him again after all they'd shared, he ached with it.

Kisa murmured as she brushed off her black leotard, speaking Russian as they always did when they talked only to each other. "With that face, everyone will guess very quickly." She glanced at where the other skaters gathered. "But perhaps you are only being paranoid. If you stay away from home, what can they really do now? They are powerless. Why not just live your life?"

A lock of Kisa's blonde hair had come loose from her ponytail, and Misha tucked it behind her ear. "You know why. You still live in Russia. My family still lives there. Until we are forgotten, it's too much of a risk. It's better for Dev too. Do you think he will get any more endorsements if the people know he's gay? Let alone that he and I are…"

"What, exactly?" Kisa raised a delicately sculpted brow.

Lovers? Boyfriends? More? Less? "That we are what we are. It doesn't matter—you know why we must keep it a secret. We may not be competing anymore, but we are still in the skating world. There are rules, even if they are not written down."

Kisa sighed and tugged his hand. "True enough. Come, we must be polite."

They skated over to the other side of the rink, passing rows of empty seats. The boards had been removed so chairs could be placed on ice level for the diehard fans willing to pay for them. High above, the lighting crews worked on scaffolding.

Dev, his partner Bailey, and a few other new arrivals were hugging the skaters who had been in Tokyo for two days. Dev's back was turned as he greeted Hanako Hirano, the young Japanese woman who was the Olympic gold medalist. Dev's hoodie stretched across his back, and his jeans clung to his lean, muscular legs.

To not be able to touch Dev and hold him close was a physical ache in Misha's chest. Dev's black curls had been cropped close, and Misha clenched his hands so he wouldn't unthinkingly reach out. He and Kisa waited on the outskirts of the group.

Bailey's fiery hair was pulled up under a baseball cap, and there were visible circles under her eyes. She and the other new arrivals stood by the edge of the ice in their sneakers. "I just want to note that your Canadians Brad and Ari are late too, Alice! It's not our fault that hurricane delayed our flight for two days. Or was it a cyclone? And what's the difference, anyway?"

"I think it's the same thing?" Brad Chang, an ice dancer and new Olympic champion, frowned at his partner. "Ari, didn't you see something on Discovery about that?"

Ariane Gagnon rubbed a hand over her face. Her brown hair was lank around her face. "I dunno. I barely remember my own name right now." She muttered something in French.

Chuckling, Brad slung his arm around her shoulders. Like most ice dancers, they were only a few inches apart in height. "Alice, I think we need some coffee, stat." He glanced over at Misha and Kisa. "Hey, guys!"

All eyes turned to them, and the crowd parted so they could skate to the end of the ice. Brad was holding up his hand, and Misha slapped it before they hugged. He gave Ariane a peck on the cheek and turned to Dev and Bailey. He met Dev's gaze and immediately glanced away, his stomach somersaulting and groin tightening.

Bailey smiled and waved awkwardly in the sudden silence. "Hi, Mikhail. Kisa. Great to see you."

Misha didn't think he could bear to touch Dev at all in front of the dozen or so people. He nodded, lifting his lips in a brief smile. "Hello."

Kisa nodded as well.

Alice cleared her throat. "Okay, so time to get back to practice. Scott, Dev, Bailey, Brad, and Ariane, I wish we had time for you guys to shower and nap, but the first show is tomorrow night, and I don't have to tell you expectations from this audience will be high. I need everyone on their game. I've got enough gray hair already. We're all going to work together as a team, right?"

They all nodded, and Brad grinned. "Alice, do you actually have any hair that isn't already gray?"

With a fake scowl, Alice skated to center ice with elegant strides. At almost sixty, she was still a graceful and long-legged skater, her silver hair pulled back in a knot. A seven-time Canadian pairs champion and two-time world champion, she had been one of the top choreographers in the world for years. Misha did enjoy working with her—even if he'd rather not be skating at all.

"Newcomers get changed. Everyone else over here. You're going to show them what we've worked on so far, and then they can join in."

As the afternoon wore on, Misha tried to concentrate. Learning group numbers was part of doing any tour, and he could pick up the moves in his sleep. He went through the motions, watching Dev from the corner of his eye, remembering their last real conversation a few days ago. Like most of their phone calls since they left LA, it had ended with Misha on his back in bed, stroking himself, his phone tucked between his cheek and shoulder.

"I can't wait to touch you again. I'm going to fuck your ass so hard you won't be able to sit down for a week."

Misha groaned. "Da. I want it so much."

"What do you want? Tell me."

"Your cock. Inside me. Coming inside me. Filling me up until it's dripping out of me."

Dev's breathing hitched. "Yeah. I'm going to fuck you raw, and you're going to love it. I bet your legs are spread so wide right now. Are you fucking yourself yet?"

Misha sucked his finger loudly and reached down to push at his hole. "I am now."

Dev panted harshly. "You love it, don't you? We need to Skype so I can see you. God, I miss you so much. Fuck, I'm coming—inside you, all over you—"

"Mikhail!" Alice's voice vibrated with tension.

Blinking, Misha realized all eyes were on him and that Kisa was pulling his hand. She glared up at him before smiling at Alice.

"Please forgive. He is not feeling well. He didn't want to cause a fuss, but he feels cold coming on. He took some medicine, and now his brain is very…fuzzy, I think you would say? Do not worry. We will be ready for the show."

Alice nodded. "I know you will. You're not Olympic champions for nothing. All right, everyone take ten, and we're going from the top."

Most of the skaters put on their plastic guards over their blades and clomped to the backstage area, eagerly reaching for their phones and flopping down on couches. While Kisa tapped away, Misha perched on the arm of the couch beside her, knowing it was a terrible idea to text Dev in front of everyone.

Dev and Bailey trailed in, still talking about their part in the opening number.

American women's champion Hallie Mitchell glanced up from her phone. "Hey, Dev. A little birdie told me you might be working in LA with Farley Clark after the summer."

Dev swigged from a bottle of water. "Yeah, I might help out a bit. See how it goes."

At the thought of being back in LA with Dev, in a house together on the beach far away from anyone who knew them, Misha couldn't hide his smile.

"But the weird thing is that I heard Mikhail was the one who set it up or something."

Misha's smile vanished as all eyes swung to him. He shrugged. "They wanted me, but I am not interested. They asked who I thought might be. I gave a few names. That is all."

Before Hallie could ask anything else, Zoloto raced toward him, shaking off rain. Her wrinkled and droopy French bulldog face made her look quite sad, while really she was the happiest little dog he'd ever known. She was almost all white, and Misha bent to scratch behind her pink ears, smiling at the PA who'd been tasked with minding her. "I hope she has been a very good girl?"

The young man nodded vigorously, and Misha was sure that

even if Zoloto had pissed over everything, the boy would never say a word. Zoloto suddenly barked excitedly and scampered off before Misha could grab her, leaping at Dev's feet. Dev scooped her up and kissed her head.

"Hey there!" He smiled nervously. "Uh, who's this?"

One of the other skaters laughed. "Zoloto, our tour mascot. Wow, she sure loves you at first sight!"

Dev avoided Misha's gaze. "Isn't she friendly with everyone?"

"Of course she is." Kisa stood and plucked Zoloto from Dev's arms. "Aren't you, *sladenkaya*." She passed her back to Misha.

A few of the skaters exchanged glances, and Bailey spoke up. "Okay, if I don't get another caffeine infusion, I'm going to face-plant out there. Come on, people. Hook me up."

Most of the skaters shuffled off toward the food table. Zoloto whined as Dev walked away.

"I know how you feel," Misha whispered, kissing and petting her, certain this day would never end.

WITH A DEEP breath, Misha put his eye to the peephole. No movement. He listened intently. The hallway was silent.

He quickly took a last look in the mirror over the dresser, fiddling with his short brown hair where it fell a bit longer over his forehead. He'd shaved and moisturized and dressed in jeans and a simple long-sleeved T-shirt that accentuated his muscles and lean hips quite nicely he thought. He stepped back for a final look. Perhaps the purple would bring out the blue in his eyes more, although the dark brown also suited him, and—

"*Dostatochno!*" Enough, enough, enough. He was behaving like a teenager.

As he eased open the door, Zoloto snorted, and he froze. But she slept on, and he slipped from the room. He was only a few doors down when Hanako appeared from the elevator with a soft *beep* and swish of doors.

She smiled brightly. "Good evening." As always, Hanako was unfailingly polite. "How are you feel?"

Misha smiled. "Better."

"Please tell if you need…" She paused, clearly struggling for the right English word. "Any things." She smiled again. As the tour headliner, she went out of her way to make sure the skaters were all happy and looked after.

He held up a padded bucket. "Just getting ice. That is all."

"Ah." She smiled and nodded deeply. "See you tomorrow."

He nodded back as they passed each other, and he made his way to the ice room at the end of the hall. He filled the bucket, relieved he'd thought to bring it. When he peeked out, the hall was empty. He'd passed Dev's room on his way, and when he neared it again, the door creaked open.

Misha ducked inside, and a moment later, he was pressed back against the door, ice cubes scattered over the plush carpet as he and Dev kissed. Dev was already naked, and Misha touched him greedily, hands roving as he groaned. "Oh God. A month is too long, *Vassenka*."

Dev sucked on Misha's neck, his light beard scratching wonderfully against Misha's skin. He muttered as he yanked on Misha's T-shirt. "I don't know what that means, but it's been an eternity. Thirty-three days, to be exact."

All Misha could do was moan as they stumbled to the bed and got rid of his clothes. He bit his lip, the feel of their already-fevered skin sliding together making him want to scream the hotel down. Dev's hair was still wet from a shower, and Misha gripped his damp curls as Dev sucked his nipples and rolled on top of him.

Rutting together like boys, they gasped, hard and leaking. "It was the worst practice ever. All day I longed to feel you," Misha mumbled. "I could not think of anything else."

"Me either." Dev gripped Misha's hips and thrust against him. "I need you so bad. God, I missed the taste of you." He licked at the hollow of Misha's throat.

Misha wanted Dev inside him already, but he was too desperate to deal with lube and a condom. He kissed Dev deeply, their tongues stroking. "Come all over me."

Above him, Dev's eyes darkened, his nostrils flaring. "You want that?"

"*Da, pozhaluysta*. Please. Hurry." Misha gasped out the words.

Dev pressed himself up on one arm so he could reach for his cock. Misha watched as the head disappeared into Dev's fist, the foreskin pulled back. Dev's body strained as he jerked himself roughly, his nipples hard, muscles straining.

"*Krasavetcs*. Beautiful. I want to look at you forever." Misha ran his hands over Dev's trembling shoulders.

Breathing loudly in the stillness of the room, Dev worked himself. "Won't take long," he muttered. "Been half hard all day. Fuck, it's so good to see you, Misha."

"Oh yes. That's it." He could watch Dev for hours but didn't want to wait tonight. "Are you going to come for me?"

"Yes!" Dev shuddered as he spurted. He striped Misha's chest and belly and then aimed for his face with jerks of his thick cock.

Misha flicked out his tongue to lick up the pearly drops near his mouth and on his chin, savoring the musky flavor. He swiped his cheek with his finger and sucked it clean.

Pupils blown, Dev leaned down to kiss him messily. Then he crawled down the bed and swallowed Misha's red, straining cock. Misha spread his legs farther and watched as Dev's cheeks hollowed, his lips stretched. Misha couldn't stop himself from lifting his hips, and Dev held him down, sucking harder.

He didn't stop sucking as he reached behind Misha's balls to tease at his hole. The feel of Dev touching him there again was all it took, and Misha pulled on Dev's hair until Dev popped off.

Misha's cock slapped against Dev's chin, and he took hold of his shaft as his orgasm tore through him.

Dev opened his mouth, and Misha aimed for it, splashing Dev's cheeks and up onto his forehead, his milky cum pale on Dev's skin. They were marking each other like animals, and it made Misha come so hard. Dev's eyes were closed, and he swallowed every drop he managed to catch.

Then they were kissing again, and the taste of them both mixed on their tongues. They were sticky and sweaty and together, and Misha had never been happier as he licked Dev's face clean. Dev ran his fingers through the mess on Misha's belly and wiped it over the lines of the tattoo on Misha's hip. Carefully, Dev traced the eagle's wings with his spunk before following with his tongue as Misha shuddered.

Breathing heavily, Dev finally flopped onto his back. "You're the best jet-lag remedy ever. You should bottle that. Although no, on second thought, I want it all for myself." He idly caressed Misha's thigh. "God, you're amazing."

Misha shrugged and tried not to smile. "Yes. This is true."

"And as modest as ever." Dev laughed before yawning widely.

"You are tired." Misha curled on his side, sliding his leg over Dev's. Drawing his fingertips over the hair on Dev's chest, he kissed his shoulder. "Perhaps we should have waited. It will be a long day tomorrow."

Eyes drifting shut, Dev shook his head. "No way. I waited long enough to have you again. No one else even comes close."

Misha's heart skipped a beat, and his hand froze on Dev's chest. The question came out before he could stop himself. "Have there been others since I saw you?" His stomach clenched at the thought.

Dev's eyes snapped open. "What? No, of course not." Hurt flickered across his face. "Have you...?"

"No." They were both rigid, and Misha soothed his hand over

Dev's chest, breathing deeply. He leaned over and kissed Dev softly. "There is only you."

With a long exhale, Dev relaxed. "Good." He rubbed their noses together. "I guess we should have talked about that, huh? I just figured we were on the same page."

"Yes. The same page. The same sentence, I think."

"Same word." Dev grinned before his smile faded. "Hey, you didn't bring Zoloto. I miss her."

"Sorry, but tonight you are all mine, Vassenka."

Dev nuzzled Misha's cheek. "Tell me what that means."

"It does not mean a thing, really. We do not have your name in Russian. But Devassy, it is a little like Vasiliy or Vassya, so...Vassenka. My little name for you." He kissed Dev lightly. "If you do not like it, I will stop."

"No, no. I like it. I like it a lot." He smiled. "Just as long as you're not secretly calling me an asshole."

"Never. Well, perhaps from time to time."

They laughed, and Dev rubbed his calf against Misha's leg. Misha played with the hair on Dev's chest. "Do you ever wear your tiny elephant?"

"After Worlds, I gave it to my mom. She was worried about some tests the doctor did, and I told her that little jade necklace would be her good-luck charm too."

"Tests? You did not mention this." Misha frowned. "Is everything all right?"

"Absolutely. She passed with flying colors." Dev smiled.

"Good, good." Misha was relieved, but there was also a twinge of sadness that Dev hadn't told him about it. But why should he? She was fine, and there was no reason Dev should tell him every small thing.

"I'm so glad I'm finally here. Damn hurricane."

"I checked the weather so often Kisa threatened to take away my phone." Misha's chest was sticky but he liked the sensation as it tightened on his skin. "I am very happy now. The whole summer we shall be together. And fall and winter and spring."

Dev ran his fingers over Misha's arm where it lay across his waist. "It's weird, isn't it? Not going back to training? Usually after Stars on Ice, it would be a week of vacation and then back to the rink. Meeting with the choreographers for new programs. Seamstress for new costumes. Then work, work, work to get ready for the fall. It's going to be so strange not to be at Skate America this year."

"It is finally over." Misha sighed with a smile.

Dev shifted onto his side facing Misha. "You sound so glad. Won't you miss it at all?"

"I would much rather be here in your bed than on the rink in Moscow."

With a chuckle, Dev kissed him. "*Duh*. But sometimes I still can't believe it's all over." His smile faded. "I know it's different for you. Now you can leave Russia." He caressed Misha's cheek. "They can't control you anymore."

His chest tightened. "I hope they will not try now that we have given them gold. My family tells me not to worry about them, but things have become worse. Many arrests. Threats. Intimidation. The government says it is all to protect children, but they lie."

"I'm so glad you left." Dev exhaled sharply. "God, it's so horrible what's happening over there."

"They were very angry when I refused to do a Russian tour. We said we had already committed to other tours. It was true enough. I hope that before long, they will forget about me. As long as I stay out of the papers, they should. There will be more skaters for them to control."

Dev grimaced. "Yeah. I think it's best if no one finds out about us for the time being. Best for Bailey and Kisa too. We have to think of them. The illusion of romance is part of pairs skating.

If people knew about us, would they still buy me and Bailey skating to some Celine Dion love song? We all need to make money doing shows while we can. Never know when the offers will dry up. There's no pro circuit the way there used to be. And you know how gossip spreads like a rash in skating. It's better to fly under the radar. Not rock the boat."

It was, although Misha wished it could be different. "What about your family?"

Dev rolled away and stared at the ceiling. "I haven't told them yet. I just...they're okay with me being gay. They are. But I've never really been serious about anyone, and I think that's made it easier for them. You know what I mean? Like, it's easier to accept that I'm gay in theory as opposed to reality. My mom has tried to set me up with guys, but she knows I won't do blind dates, so it's safe. I worry about how my parents will react if I..." He looked at Misha. "If *we*..."

Misha nodded. "Right now, it can be our secret, yes? Let us see how we feel after the summer." He ran his thumb over Dev's lower lip. "Part of me wishes I could scream from the rooftops how I care for you." He chuckled. "Everyone would be very shocked, I think. They believe we hate each other very much."

"They definitely do." Dev laughed. "In the shuttle to the hotel tonight, Brad was all, 'Wow, those Russians haven't thawed out, huh?'" He traced the contours of Misha's face with his fingertip. "If only he knew how hot you are. How passionate."

Desire sparked in Misha's belly, and Dev's light touch sent a shiver down his spine. "It is enough that you know. It is just ours for now. Well, and Kisa and Bailey. And Zoloto. No one else needs to know until we decide."

Dev's lips quirked up. "I'm just imagining the looks on people's faces. I think the Feds would have a group heart attack. By the way, they tried to convince me and Bailey to un-retire. Sue Stabler was at her most charming and persuasive when she came to see us on Stars on Ice."

Misha's breath caught. "Your federation wants you to continue?" A barrage of thoughts tumbled through his mind. Dev moving back to Colorado Springs to train. Traveling around the world to compete. Misha only seeing him a few times a year. *No, no, no.*

"Hey, hey." Dev held Misha closer. "It's okay. Bailey and I are done. We decided that last year. We're going to do shows and get all the money we can before America forgets about us. And we're going to enjoy the hell out of not being up at five a.m. every day to train."

With an exhale, Misha relaxed again. "Okay."

"We get to travel Asia together all summer, and then we'll find a house right by the water in LA. I loved that one rental listing you e-mailed." His eyelids drooped. "Looks perfect."

"I thought so also." Misha smiled.

Dev's eyes closed. "Mmm."

"Comfortable?" Misha pulled the thick covers over them.

"Uh-huh. I think..." Dev trailed off, his lips parting.

Misha kissed Dev's forehead. "I think you sleep now."

For a long while, he closed his eyes and listened to Dev's soft snores. He knew he had to return to his own room and that they would be together again the next night. And the next and the next and the next. But he snuggled in closer. Soon he would go, but not just yet.

Chapter Twelve

"*Chert,*" Misha muttered as he dug his phone out of the wet sand. That's what he got for keeping it in the pocket of his hoodie and not his jeans.

Zoloto circled him, barking before scurrying away from an incoming wave. Misha hurried back to the house while she trotted along behind. After climbing the few stairs to the wooden patio and rinsing his feet with a low tap, Misha left her gnawing on a rubber bone while he slipped inside and slid the glass door shut behind him. Better to deal with the phone without her underfoot.

The sun warmed the pantry of the bright, open kitchen. Misha pulled out the bag of brown rice and filled a plastic container, nestling his damp phone inside. With any luck, the rice would soak up the moisture. As he sealed the lid carefully, Dev's voice echoed down from upstairs.

"Hey, Ma."

The main-floor living room had a cathedral ceiling, with the three bedrooms upstairs tucked away at the front and back of the house. The master bedroom faced the sea with floor-to-ceiling windows, and Dev used one of the guest rooms as a sort of office. He was likely there now, and Misha wondered whether he should go and tempt Dev away from work. He smiled to himself. It was late afternoon—surely he needed a break.

"Work's going really well. I'm learning a lot from Mr. Clark. I was just tweaking the practice plans for the junior skaters." He paused. "Of course he knows I'm doing the show in Boston on Christmas Eve. Ma, he has no problem with giving me time off to do shows. Yes, I know NBC is actually airing live skating for the first time in forever. No, it's not a problem. Yes, I'm sure. Yes, I'll be prepared to skate. Mr. Clark has a few other assistants, and I'm the low man on the totem pole."

Misha smiled to himself. Dev might be new at coaching, but he was a natural. Misha had no doubt Dev would have his own students one day.

"What do you mean, Ma? I'm only working part time, and he's good with that. Yes, I'll be home next week for rehearsals." He paused again. "No, they're putting us up in a hotel by the Garden. Because it'll be a heck of a lot easier than coming in from Belmont every day. And before you ask, *yes*, of course I'm staying for Christmas. I'm not sure about New Year's yet. But you know me. It's my least favorite holiday. Much ado about nothing."

Misha stopped in the doorway of the kitchen. He'd wanted to be back in LA by the thirty-first so they could do something special together. Since they were still keeping their relationship to themselves, he'd thought he would cook dinner—some of the traditional holiday dishes from home. Maybe get a New Year's tree, as they'd have in Russia. Yet, perhaps Dev would not want to celebrate.

Misha tried not to feel disappointed but failed miserably. It would feel very sad not to celebrate the new year. Even when he trained in Moscow, he and Kisa and their coaches always had a tree and special dinner.

"Wait, what? Ma, you're not setting me up." A pause. "I don't care if he's a cardiologist! I'm not interested."

Misha knew he should go back outside with Zoloto, but he couldn't seem to stop listening to Dev's voice from upstairs.

"Because...because I'm seeing someone already."

Misha's heart skipped a beat.

Dev sighed loudly. "Calm down. Of course I was going to tell you. I'm telling you right now!"

Would Dev really finally tell his mother he was living with his most hated rival? Yes, they'd agreed to keep it secret, but months had gone by. Misha knew they'd both been afraid that in the real world their connection wouldn't last, but Misha had never been so happy.

He held his breath, knowing he shouldn't eavesdrop but frozen on the spot anyway.

From upstairs, Dev went on. "It's someone from…skating. From the rink. So I don't need you to set me up." A hush. "His name? It's…Misha. Ma, I have to go. There's another call. Love you!"

In the silence that followed, Dev didn't speak to anyone else. Misha remained in the kitchen doorway, watching the sunlight dapple the light-wood flooring that ran through the house. He understood Dev's hesitation to tell his mother the truth, but his chest still felt hollow. At least Dev had given his name, although Mrs. Avira would only know him—and dislike him—as Mikhail. The man who'd beaten her son and stolen his dream of Olympic gold.

Dev was on the stairs when Misha snapped out of his reverie. He quickly retreated and opened the large stainless-steel fridge. When Dev walked in, Misha glanced over, and butterflies frolicked in his belly as Dev smiled.

"Hey! Good walk?" Dev kissed him easily, his hand trailing over Misha's hip.

"Except for dropping my phone." Misha motioned to the plastic container on the counter. "They say to seal it in rice and not to turn it on. We shall see."

"Shit. I'm sorry." Dev bent and peered into the side of the clear container. He chuckled. "I have no idea what I'm expecting to see. But if you need a new phone, I'm pretty sure I can get a deal with adding someone else to my plan."

"Even though we are not…official?" Misha opened the produce drawer in the fridge and rooted around aimlessly.

"Well, we can tell the phone company we live together. I'm pretty sure they won't send out a press release." He rubbed his palm across Misha's back. "Hey, are you okay? Don't worry about the phone. We'll sort it out."

"Of course." Misha waved his hand dismissively and kept his tone light. He had agreed that Dev could tell his family in his own time, and there was no sense in being upset. He stepped back so Dev could see into the fridge as well. "What shall we eat?"

"Whatever you want. I'm easy."

Misha smirked. "Yes, but what are you hungry for?"

Dev nudged him with his shoulder. "Ha, ha."

"We could go out. I have read about a new Italian restaurant only a few blocks away."

Dev tensed. "But what if someone sees us? With smartphones now, it's pretty easy to get caught. I think it's better that we stay in. Don't you?"

"Ya, ya." Misha shrugged. "It was only an idea."

"Hey," Dev murmured as he rubbed Misha's back. "Are you upset? You know it's not that I don't want to. If you've changed your mind about keeping this quiet, tell me."

"No, of course not. Nothing has changed in our situation. But we had dinner in Annecy and no one discovered us. Remember? Up in the mountains?"

Dev smiled tenderly. "I remember. One day we'll go back there. In the meantime…"

"Yes." Misha pressed a kiss to Dev's cheek. "All right, what shall we eat?"

"You know I never met food I didn't like."

"You did not like the borscht."

"I did!" Dev slapped his arm lightly. "Just because I didn't have seconds, you're convinced I hated it. Besides, you didn't even like it!"

Misha huffed. "Of course I did!"

"You did not and you know it. You only made it as a joke anyway."

Truthfully, it had been watery, and Misha needed his mother's recipe and not the thing he'd found online. "Perhaps," he allowed.

"Ah! Finally he admits it!"

"I admit nothing, Vassenka." Misha tried not to smile. He plucked the carton of milk from the fridge, shooting Dev a glare when he felt how empty it was. "Why do you put it back with only a few drops left?"

"There's plenty left!" Dev took the carton from him and shook it. "Well, okay. Maybe not. I'll pick up more tomorrow. But hey, you left the lid off the toothpaste this morning. *Again.* Just FYI."

"Many apologies. I suppose I must have one flaw, no?"

Dev smacked Misha's ass playfully. "I suppose. Okay, dinner. No borscht. But no cake tonight either. We've got to fit into our costumes in two weeks. Not that you'll have any trouble, always running around the beach." He patted his stomach. "But if I'm not careful, the five pounds I've gained is going to become ten."

Misha pulled Dev close and ran his hands over the firm, lean muscles beneath Dev's T-shirt. "You are too critical. None of us stay at competition weight. We should eat and be happy. Although we still have to lift the girls, so let's hope they have not been *too* happy."

Dev laughed. "I dare you to say that to Kisa."

"I value my good health far too much." He picked an apple from amid the tangerines and bananas in a bowl on the island in the middle of the kitchen. "Did I mention she wants me to...how do you say it? Gift her away? At her wedding."

"Give her away. That's great. But wait, does that mean you'd go back to Russia for the wedding? Are you sure it would be okay?" Frowning, Dev ran his hand up and down Misha's arm. "Do you think the officials who know you're gay would try to use it against you? With all the arrests happening, I don't think you should go back."

Misha played with the stem of the apple, trying to keep his voice casual. "Kisa says it will be a long engagement so that I may attend. With more time, the people will forget about me and I won't be of any consequence to the government. That is my great hope, at least. And that this government will fall and reason and justice will return."

"I hope so too. I'm sorry you have to deal with this and be so far away from your family." Dev kissed him softly. "I meant to tell you that I was thinking…"

"Were you? That only leads to no good."

Dev smiled and ignored him. "I was thinking I can get to know Kisa more this time. And you and Bailey too. On tour, we avoided each other so much in public that the four of us never really hung out."

Misha raised an eyebrow. "Are we sure this is such good idea?"

"Bailey and Kisa will get along great. Once they get to know each other. Probably. Maybe."

"I suppose we will hope for the best, yes?"

"Yes." Dev kissed him lightly. "Now let's make dinner and watch the next disc of *Buffy*. We're getting close to the end of season two, and it's *awesome*."

"Is there more Spike? He's delicious."

"He'll be back, don't worry. I'm more of an Angel guy myself. Hey, why don't we grill that zucchini and a couple of steaks?"

Misha nodded, smiling as Dev pulled the meat from the freezer, humming. There was a plaintive scratching at the door in the living room, and he went to open it for Zoloto, who greeted him as a father long lost.

IN THE BAREST glimmer of a crescent moon, the dark waves broke and rolled to shore. Misha leaned his forehead against the cool glass of the floor-to-ceiling window. He could watch the ocean for days and never tire of it. Behind him, Dev stirred with a snort and mumble.

Dev's voice was sleep slurred. "You okay?"

"Yes. Only thinking."

There was a smile in Dev's voice. "That only leads to no good."

After the whisper of sheets and creak of the mattress, he was there, lips soft on the nape of Misha's neck. They were both naked, and Misha shivered as Dev caressed his ass while his other hand stole around to stroke Misha's chest and he pressed close.

"What's up? Aside from you at three fifteen in the morning."

Leaning back into Dev's warmth and the security of his arms, Misha closed his eyes to the sea. "It feels like such a dream sometimes. Being here. Being with you. Some nights I think when next I open my eyes, it will all have vanished and I'll be back in Moscow in that tiny apartment. With only practice, practice, practice. Nothing but ice forever."

Dev's hands were gentle. "It's over now. You're here. You're safe."

Misha sighed. "Da."

After a silence, Dev spoke softly. "It's still strange sometimes. After all those years, the same routine every season. Right now we'd be exhausted from the Grand Prix circuit, and you'd have Russian Nationals next week while I'd try to squeeze Christmas into my training schedule. Sometimes I wake up and for a moment I panic because I think I must have slept in and my coach is going to kill me."

Misha chuckled. "Yes. Very strange at times. As though we are playing make-believe. Hiding from our true lives." Misha shuddered as the vestige of a dream whipped through his head. "Sometimes I fear a bang on the door. That they will come to take me away."

"But you kept up your end of the bargain. The KGB or whatever the hell they're calling themselves these days don't have any power over you. Not since you won the gold."

Opening his eyes, Misha tried to see Dev's face in their moonlit reflection on the glass, but there were only the waves. He caught Dev's fingers in his own and raised his hand for a kiss. They'd barely spoken of it since the Games, but he knew the silver medal would always be a disappointment for Dev. He had a passion for skating that had died in Misha years ago when officials had forced him back to train in Russia. "I wish you could have won."

Dev's laugh was a harsh burst of warmth on the back of Misha's neck, and his body tensed. "No you don't."

He held onto Dev's hand and sighed. "Perhaps not. But part of me wishes it. Truly."

"And part of me is glad you won." He wrapped his arms around Misha's waist, the tension dissipating as quickly as it came. "And a big part of me still can't believe we're here together. A year ago I would have said the odds of me living with Mikhail Reznikov in a beach house in Santa Monica were about a bazillion to one."

"Is that more than a billion?"

"Clearly." Dev nipped Misha's shoulder.

"Will I meet your parents in Boston?" Misha blurted out the question before he could stop himself.

Dev went still, his arms around Misha's middle. "Do you want to meet them?"

"Yes. Perhaps. I don't know."

"I thought we agreed. We both said it was better this way. At least at first." His hands dropped away as he stepped back.

Misha faced him and reached out to brush a wayward curl from Dev's forehead. "It's getting long again."

"I'm getting it cut next week before the show. Misha, don't change the subject." Dev frowned. "Am I wrong? We said we'd keep this private until…until I don't know when. I just don't know if my parents are ready for this yet."

"My parents know about you."

"I know." Dev blew out a long breath. "It's not that I don't want to tell them. I just want to make sure it's the right time. Which I realize sounds incredibly lame. But it's…complicated." He rubbed his face. "There's so much to learn at work, and we have the show coming up. It makes me nauseous to think about telling my family right now."

"It's all right. It's your choice." Misha petted Dev's hair. "Don't be upset."

"It feels so safe here with you. I don't want everyone else and their bullshit to ruin it. Not while we're still figuring everything out. You're not even sure what you want to do."

"I thought I might…" He shook his head. "It is silly, really."

"What is it?" Dev ran his hands over Misha's sides. "Tell me. Please?"

"The other week I started writing. I brought my laptop outside to answer e-mail, and I found myself with words to say. A story about a boy in a castle with dragons and giants. See? It's foolishness. I have always made up these stories in my mind, but who would want to read about such things?"

"Me, for starters. And lots of people. If you want to be a writer—write. Go for it. What do you have to lose? I think it would be amazing."

"Yes?" Excitement sang in Misha's veins. "Although I will have to write in Russian. My English spelling is not so good. You really think this would be a worthy thing?"

"Absolutely." Dev kissed him. "And about my parents...I do want you to meet my family. Once my mom gets over the fact that she's resented you for years, she's totally going to love you."

He chuckled. "Hmm. Yes, perhaps we wait. It is as you said—complicated."

"They'll be at the show on Christmas Eve. You could meet them then. Show them what a nice guy you are, so when I do tell them, it won't be such a shock. So that means you have to be the real you. Not skating you."

He frowned. "I am real as a skater."

Dev rolled his eyes. "You're aloof and cold and perfect as a skater. There's a reason we called you Robot Reznikov." He ran his hands over Misha's ass. "If people only knew what you're really like." He nipped Misha's neck, his breath hot. "How you are when we're together. I love being here with you. It's better than I ever dreamed."

"Truly?" Misha's chest felt so full of his heart he could hardly breathe.

"Of course." Dev kissed Misha gently. "I love it here. I love my new job." He huffed out a laugh. "It's funny, you know. Only Bailey knows about you, but I've never been so committed to someone. We live together. We don't see anyone else. I don't even know why we use condoms anymore."

Excitement bolted through Misha, everything else forgotten. "You want this too? Sex with...only us? No rubber?"

Dev nodded, his breath coming shallowly. "I know I'm clean. Had all the tests for the tour insurance. You did too, right?"

"Yes. It is safe." Misha's fingers tingled and he licked his lips. "I want this very much. I wasn't sure if you...if you would..." It had been part of their fantasies when they'd had phone sex, but the real thing was different.

Dev brushed back Misha's short hair where it swooped over his forehead. "I've never trusted anyone the way I trust you."

"*Ya tozhe*," Misha murmured. "Me either. How I would love to feel you come." He grazed his teeth over Dev's earlobe. "Love to have you fill me with nothing between us. Love…"

Yet, he hesitated to say the words properly. He loved Dev. This he knew without doubt. He thought Dev loved him as well, but neither of them spoke it.

Then Dev was kissing him, and Misha stopped thinking. They stumbled to the bed, lips and tongues and hands exploring as if their bodies were new. Dev's stubble scraped over Misha's heated skin, and the thought that he was going to have Dev inside him with no barrier between them set his blood rushing.

He rolled away to fumble for the plastic tube they kept in the small table next to the bed and slicked his fingers. Pushing onto his knees, he reached back to open himself and get ready.

Dev groaned beside him, stroking himself to full hardness as he watched. "Just like the first time. God, you're amazing. You have no idea how much I've wanted this. How much I've wanted to fuck you raw. Spread you open and fill you up until it's dripping out of you, down your thighs and—"

"Da, da! Now. Fuck me now." Misha flipped over and lifted his knees to his shoulders, opening himself.

Dev moved over him, holding his weight on his arms. "I wish you could see yourself like this. So perfect." He licked into Misha's mouth. "You're going to make me come just thinking about being inside you," he muttered.

Gripping Dev's curls, Misha tugged. "Do it. Fuck me. *Voydi v menya*. Inside me."

Their eyes met as Dev pushed at Misha's hole, the stretch sweet as the head nudged inside. Without a condom, Misha felt Dev's cock like a brand, and he moaned over and over. "Da. *Ya goryu dlya tebya*. Burning for you, Vassenka. More, more."

With a powerful thrust of his hips, Dev was inside him, pushing so deep that Misha was sure he'd break in two—and die happy. He raised his legs onto Dev's shoulders, squeezing around his cock.

Panting, Dev grabbed Misha's hips, heavy on top of him. "You feel so good. Jesus, it's so good. I can feel every inch of you. Fuck, Misha."

It was hard to breathe, being bent in half as he was, and Misha gasped, his mouth open as he rocked with Dev's thrusts. "Fuck me forever. I love your cock. Fill me until there's nothing left."

Their flesh slapped together as Dev drove into him, and Misha reveled in the hot pleasure spiking through his body as Dev hit the perfect place and in the freedom to be truly himself, open and bare.

Sweat beaded on Dev's face, and Misha licked it, their teeth clashing as they rutted together, trying to kiss. Everywhere Dev's body touched him, Misha was on fire, but nowhere more than in his core, Dev's cock like the most exquisite hot iron, scorching him and making him whole at the same time.

"I'm so close," Dev muttered. "Jesus. So good."

Misha teased Dev's nipples, knowing it would send him over the edge.

Groaning, Dev batted his hand away. "You first." He reached between them and jerked Misha's dick, his hips still hammering Misha's ass. "Come for me, Misha. Just me."

"Only you, Vassenka," he agreed, shaking as his balls drew up. When Dev rubbed against the right spot inside him again, Misha came apart, his ankles by his ears as he cried out. He was flying, grounded only by Dev's cock deep inside him. He clamped down as he splashed between them, and Dev gasped.

"Oh God!" He threw his head back, muscles straining as he came.

Deep within, Misha could feel Dev's release as though it marked him like ink, and he squeezed hard, milking out every drop until it did drip from his ass. He had never felt anything like it before. It was messy and wet and entirely wonderful. He dragged Dev's head down for a kiss, both of them panting and trembling.

When Dev slowly pulled out, Misha whimpered at the loss, his legs still bent back. Sitting back on his heels, lips parted, Dev dipped his fingers into Misha's stretched hole, mesmerized. Misha took hold of Dev's wrist and brought up his hand to suck his sticky fingers clean.

Exhaling noisily, Dev shook his head. "So good," he whispered. "We should have done this months ago." He gently lowered Misha's legs, kissing his knees gently as he did. "You're incredible."

"You fuck me like I've always dreamed of."

His dark eyes fiercely intent, Dev kissed him deeply. "Always." Sighing, he nuzzled Misha's neck. "About before...are we good?"

Everything they'd talked about seemed so distant and unimportant. "We are better than good, Vassenka."

They fell asleep sated and sprawled, and Misha's last thought was of how soon they could do it again.

Chapter Thirteen

"So."

Misha smiled awkwardly. "Yes. Here we are."

He gazed at the people crowding around the arrivals gate. In the twenty seconds since Dev had left to go to the bathroom, Misha had tried to think of something to say and had come up empty. Bailey smiled back up at him. Like most female pairs skaters, she was very petite, not even reaching Misha's shoulder. As a family pushing an overloaded luggage cart shoved through the crowd, she stepped closer.

"We are indeed."

"It was very kind of you to come and for Dev to borrow his father's car. The producers were surprised when I told them Kisa wouldn't need transportation."

"I bet. Guess you didn't tell them who was picking her up."

"No. I omitted that part." Looking up at the arrivals board, Misha pointed. "Should be any minute. Probably a line at customs."

"Yeah, the airport's really busy this time of year."

Another silence. Then Misha asked, "Your parents will be in California for Christmas? Your brother lives in San Francisco?"

"Yep. His wife just had another baby, and they're all super excited. It sucks I can't be there, but this show on Christmas Eve should be cool. NBC's all into live specials these days. If the ratings are good, maybe skating can make it back into prime time on a regular basis."

He wasn't sure what prime time meant but nodded. "That would be good, yes."

"How's the dog? Where's she staying while you guys are here?"

"The neighbor next door. She has a pug who plays with Zoloto often. At least while we are gone Zoloto can still run on the sand and feel at home. I do not like leaving her, but it's only a week or so."

They watched the arrivals and delays flash on the board.

Bailey unbuttoned her dark pea coat and put it over her arm. She wore jeans and a green turtleneck sweater that contrasted well with the red in her hair. She clapped her hands decisively. "Okay, so let's just power through this awkwardness."

Misha braced himself. "Okay."

"Since we avoided each other on tour because you and Dev have a hard time being in the same room without looking like you want to suck each other's faces, you and I have never really, you know…talked. And Dev'll be back any minute, so I just want to say that you make him really happy, and I'm glad." She rocked on her heels, her boots clacking. "That's all, I guess. I think it would be cool to be friends, because Dev's my boy and I don't want it to be weird with us."

"I would like very much to be friends. I…" He tried to find the words. "Dev makes me very happy as well."

Eyes gleaming, Bailey grinned. "He does, doesn't he? You're crazy about him. You have good taste, Mikhail. I approve."

"Misha. Please call me this. We are friends, yes?"

"Okay. Misha." She smiled again. "Sounds good."

He cast about for something else to say. For a moment they were quiet in the din of the crowd and the crackle of announcements over the loudspeaker. "Dev said you will visit in February."

"Yeah, if it's cool with you. I'll be dying for some sunshine by then. Pittsburgh in the winter? Not my favorite place."

"I have never been. But I am used to Moscow winters, so I can imagine."

"Do you miss it? Russia, I mean. Not the winters. Your family and everything. The government really sucks these days. Not that ours is much better. But the anti-gay stuff is crazy over there. It's like they really went back in time."

"I do miss it, but the last years it felt more like prison than true home." He tried to ignore the pang of sadness at the thought of his family in St. Petersburg. "There is talk of a new party to rival the government. But it might come to nothing."

Bailey grimaced. "That guy is a total dictator. He sucks."

"Yes. We hope he can be voted out, but there is so much corruption. The situation for homosexuals becomes worse and worse. So much violence and hatred."

She squeezed his arm. "I'm so glad you were able to come here."

"I am glad also. And glad you are here. Thank you for coming to the airport."

"Of course." She shrugged. "It's weird, huh? You, Kisa, me, and Dev—we've known each other for years but not really at all until now. I mean, you and Dev certainly have been getting to know each other *extremely* well the past year. But it's funny how you can be around people for years and never really know them. It's cool to talk to you about real stuff."

"I feel the same." He touched her shoulder.

"Hey, Dev said your family's visiting next year?"

"Yes, my parents and sister are coming next March. My niece and nephews as well. It will be wonderful."

"That's awesome. So...they know about Dev?"

Misha nodded. "They are excited to meet him." He was nervous and eager. He wanted it all to be perfect. "It will be a very full house, but I hope a happy one. I want to visit them, but my father tells me I should not."

"But Kisa still lives there?" Bailey asked. "Duh, obviously, since we're meeting her flight from Russia."

"Yes. When we have no shows to skate in, she is with her family, planning her marriage."

"Whoa! She's engaged? How did I miss this memo?" Bailey elbowed him playfully. "Tell me everything. Who's the guy?"

"Alexei. He teaches the little ones at the school in their town. He and Kisa have loved each other since they were young."

"*Really?* Huh." Bailey cleared her throat. "I mean, it's not that...I just...that's great! I'm so happy for her."

"It is all right. I know how Kisa seems to people. Like a bitch."

Bailey opened her mouth and shut it again. "Well, we weren't exactly braiding each other's hair in the dressing room over the years, but I'm sure she's very nice. That's great that she's engaged. Really."

"What about you? Dev says you have no boyfriend. This surprises me."

"Surprises my mother too." Bailey shrugged. "I dunno. I can't seem to find a guy who isn't a complete loser. It's a problem I have. I attract them in droves, like douchey bees to honey. But I live in hope that I'll meet a guy who doesn't completely suck."

"We all live in hope, B." Dev appeared behind them with a grin. He stood close to Misha and gave his hip an affectionate pat.

Misha smiled softly.

"Okay, you realize you two are like, super coupley, right? You hid it on tour, but now that you've been living together the past few months, you are all up in each other's space, and everyone is going to know in a nanosecond. Which I think is just fine, for the record, but since you guys want to keep it on the down-low, you'd better make like you're at a Catholic high school dance and put some daylight between you."

"Catholic...dance?" Misha asked. He struggled to keep up

with Bailey's rapid-fire way of speaking.

She waved her hand. "Just make sure you're not brushing up against each other all the time. Sweet said she heard things were super tense between all of us on tour in Asia, so you guys pulled it off then, but you'd better try harder now."

Dev added, "She means Caroline Mortimer."

"Oh sorry. Yeah, Sweet Caroline."

"Like the song," Misha said.

"You know that song?" Bailey's eyebrows shot up.

"B, he's from Russia. Not the dark side of the moon," Dev said.

She huffed. "I *know*. But it's an old song, dude. Misha doesn't strike me as a big Neil Young fan."

"Neil Diamond," Dev corrected. "Ma would be pulling out her old records right now to school you."

"Right, right. I can never keep those Neils straight. Speaking of not being able to keep straight, seriously, if you keep looking at each other like that, you might as well forget it."

"Like what?" Dev asked as he and Misha glanced at each other.

Misha smiled, and Dev smiled back.

"Like *that*." Bailey rolled her eyes. "You guys are such goners. Oh!" She pointed to the new wave of people streaming through from customs. "I think this is her flight. Look at all those fur coats."

Misha laughed at Dev's frown. "She is correct. Some stereotypes are the truth."

Bailey eyed his black leather jacket. "Where's your fur, Misha? Next time I see you, I expect you to be rocking a mink hat. Make it happen."

"I will do my best."

"But not really. I'd feel too guilty about the poor little minks. Faux fur all the way."

Dev smiled at them, and Misha knew he was pleased that they were being friendly. Misha hoped the friendliness would continue when Kisa arrived. Just then, he spotted her and waved. She edged through the crowd, pulling two huge suitcases behind her. As always, she was impeccably dressed and made up, with diamonds glittering in her ears and her blonde hair knotted at her neck. Her dark wool coat was cuffed in white fur.

She dragged up her suitcases, and Misha lifted her from the ground and squeezed her close, her weight in his arms and scent in his nose so wonderfully familiar. He placed her down and gave her a kiss before telling her he'd missed her. "*Ya skuchal po tebe.*"

"Ya tozhe."

Around them, there were murmurs, and he became aware of some of the arriving passengers from Moscow pointing to them excitedly. While in America he was only recognized very occasionally, in Russia it was quite different. He also became aware that some people were clearly discombobulated to see him and Kisa with Bailey and Dev.

Kisa turned to Bailey and Dev with a tentative smile. "Hello."

"Hi." Dev reached out uncertainly, as if torn between a handshake or something more. "It's good to see you. Um…"

Bailey gave him a nudge. "Come on, you guys. We've fake hugged a million times on the podium. We can do it for real."

Laughing, Dev and Kisa hugged briefly and Kisa kissed his cheek.

"Hey, not just an air kiss! This is serious progress," Bailey whispered to Misha. "Okay, my turn." She hugged Kisa and stepped back. "Those gold earrings are fabulous. Now show me your rock."

Kisa's brows drew together, and she glanced at Misha. "My what?"

"Oh, sorry—I mean your ring," Bailey answered.

Beaming, Kisa lifted her left hand. A square diamond sparkled on her finger. "Alexei says he saved for it since our first kiss."

Bailey whistled. "Alexei has very good taste, and that's incredibly adorable. I'm going to need pictures and all the details."

Misha and Dev glanced at each other. Dev gave a hopeful smile and reached for Kisa's bags. "Come on. You must be exhausted."

With Misha and Dev each lugging a suitcase behind them, they escaped the crowds to the parking garage. Dev had borrowed his father's Cadillac, which fortunately had a large trunk. Misha groaned as he lifted the first bag. "I see you still pack everything you own."

"A woman has needs, Misha. You men do not understand."

Bailey chimed in. "She's right. You guys may be gay, but you're still *guys*. A lady needs options."

"And *Ded Moroz* might have sent a few things for you, so don't complain, Misha." Kisa swatted him before climbing into the backseat.

Misha paused and considered whether to get into the back with Kisa, but Bailey nudged him toward the front seat. Once they were out of the labyrinth of the parking lot, Bailey piped up.

"Who's Ded Moroz? Friend of yours?"

Misha and Kisa laughed, and Misha said, "No. He is Father Cold…" He pondered the translation. "Father Frost. He is like Santa Claus."

"You have a different Santa over there? Does he still come on Christmas Eve?"

"No, on New Year's Eve. In Russia, this is the very big holiday. We have a New Year's tree, and Father Cold comes to give us presents with his granddaughter, *Snegurochka*." Misha paused again. "Snow Girl, you would call her. Christmas in Russia is not until January seventh."

"Really?" Dev asked. "Why's that?"

"We have a different calendar for religious days. So there is another New Year's on January thirteenth as well. It is the old-style New Year."

Kisa added, "We have celebration for two weeks. Misha and I could hardly take part since we were practicing for European championships at that time. But this year I will do nothing but go visiting and laugh and eat tangerines and *pelmenyi*."

"Ohh, what's that?" Bailey asked.

"Little dumplings with meat. We eat them with thick sour cream," Kisa explained.

Bailey sighed dreamily. "Isn't eating the best? Not that we can gain too much weight while we're still doing shows. But man, how awesome is not having to count every single calorie?"

"It is quite good. In a few years I will get pregnant and wonderfully fat."

"Okay, now you have to tell me everything about the future father of your children."

While Bailey chattered and Kisa answered her questions, Misha smiled to himself. He was grateful to Bailey for her kindness and the open way she could talk to people and make them at ease. He placed his hand on Dev's thigh. Dev smiled as he pulled up to a red light. He opened his mouth to say something, but his phone rang. He held up his finger to Misha and quickly answered.

"Ma? I can't talk, I'm in the car. I'll be back soon. Do you need me to pick something up?" He paused. "Got it. Of course skim. I can't believe you finally got Dad off the two percent." Another pause. "Yes, I told you I'll stay over tonight. But rehearsal starts tomorrow. Ma, the light's turning. Love you." He tapped off his phone. "Sorry."

"No need." Misha lowered his voice and leaned closer, sliding his hand higher on Dev's thigh. The girls were still talking, and Bailey was laughing uproariously about something. "I will miss you tonight."

Dev glanced at him with bright eyes. "Me too. But even if I was at the hotel, we agreed we shouldn't see each other. It's a miracle no one caught us on tour. That night in Seoul was close."

"That night was also—"

"Don't say it," Dev hissed with a laugh. He whispered, "But yes. Mind blowing. Now stop distracting me." He took Misha's hand from his leg and kissed it quickly before placing it back in Misha's lap.

With a smile, Misha tuned back in to the conversation in the backseat.

Kisa was nodding. "Yes. I feel they are very bad at hiding."

"Right?" Bailey exclaimed. "*Thank you.* I think no one suspects because it's so outside the realm of what they would ever have thought would happen. Ever. In a million years."

"I would not have bet on this happening, that is certain," Kisa said.

Bailey laughed. "Seriously, how freaking weird is this? We're all hanging out here in Dev's dad's car. But you know what? It's a good weird. Kisa, I think we should get drunk and dish about these two. This peace summit calls for vodka, and lots of it."

Misha and Dev shared a look, and Dev shook his head as he changed lanes. "Remember how we wanted them to be friends, Misha?"

"A regrettable desire," Misha answered.

"Oh yeah, this is happening. Watch out, boys." Bailey giggled.

"Extremely regrettable," Dev said with a smile.

Misha glanced back at Kisa, who gave his shoulder an affectionate squeeze. With a satisfied sigh, Misha settled back and watched the lights of Boston sail by.

"OKAY, EVERYONE!" ALICE clapped her hands. "Thank you all for being here right on time this morning. I know there's a lot of jet lag going on, so we'll ease into it. Take some time to warm up and get a feel for the ice, and then we'll start with the group opening number. It's a challenging program, but I know you're all up to the task. We're going to knock America's socks off."

Kisa was already stroking around the rink as Misha took off his skate guards. The large arena was empty but for the NBC crew working on the lighting and many producers and production assistants. The young PAs scurried around with clipboards and perpetual frowns. Misha watched Dev and Bailey skate by before forcing himself to tear his gaze away.

He pushed off from the boards and bent his knees, getting a feel for the ice. It was good—not too hard and not too soft. It had been months since he laced up, and he realized with a start that it was the longest time he'd been off the ice since he was a small boy. His shoulders tensed, and the old tightening of his chest returned as he stroked around the rink. He reached automatically for Kisa's hand, but she was on the other side of the ice.

Breathing deeply, he reminded himself that competing was over. No more judges, no more federation. He was free now, and the Russian officials didn't control him anymore. Winning Olympic gold had been his ticket to this new life, and everything was all right.

Kisa appeared at his side, and they joined hands. He smiled down at her. "Do you miss it?"

"Competition, no." She squeezed his fingers. "Skating with you, yes. Let us have fun, Misha."

As they skated around the rink, every so often they'd pass Dev and Bailey. Although he loved Kisa dearly, Misha couldn't help but wish it was Dev's hand in his. Caroline and her ice-dance partner Grant were skating arm in arm and gazing at each other with open affection.

"Romance blooms," Kisa noted.

"Yes. Bailey said they finally…let me get the words right…" He switched to English. "They finally 'hooked up' in the summer."

Kisa chuckled. "You know, Bailey also said something interesting. That you and Dev hardly go out because you are both afraid your secret will be revealed."

He shrugged. "It's not a problem. It is better to be cautious."

"For how long? Years?"

Misha's stomach churned.

"It weighs upon you, Misha. I can see it plainly. So much more than it did when we were training. You came to America to be free, but you are still hiding."

"I must. At least until…"

"When? When will the good time be?"

"Can I get Kisa, Mikhail, Bailey, and Dev over here, please?" Alice called. She and her two assistants waited in one corner of the rink.

He sighed as they skated over. "I don't know. But I'm fine. Really." He kissed her cheek and gave her shoulders a squeeze.

Once they were assembled, Alice smiled. "Hello. First off, let me just say how excited I am that you all agreed to do this show. I was thinking we could do a number with the four of you. Switching partners, skating together as a group—that kind of thing. I understand you might not be the best of friends, but the fans really love seeing rivals skate together."

For a moment, the four of them were silent.

Then Bailey piped up. "I think it's a great idea! Right, guys? It's cool, Alice. We're all professionals here." She unzipped her hoodie. They all wore plain practice gear—tank tops and spandex pants. "Let's get started."

"Absolutely," Kisa agreed with a slight nod.

Misha and Dev nodded, and Misha was aware of the many eyes on them. Apparently their act on the Asian tour truly had been a roaring success, because everyone in the arena seemed to be waiting for them to brawl on the ice. Misha had thought he would be able to keep up the pretense, but the day had barely started and he felt frayed around the edges.

Alice exhaled. "Wonderful. Let me take you through what I have in mind."

One of the producers nearby raised his hand. "Also? We've arranged a joint interview for the four of you tomorrow night at the hotel. We hope it won't be a problem."

The four of them glanced at each other, and Misha answered. "We have no problem." *Except for pretending to the reporter we are enemies.*

With a bright smile, Alice nodded to her assistants. "Okay, we'll show you what we were thinking for this routine…"

An hour later, Misha held Bailey's hands as she skated backwards and they prepared for a lift. Dev and Kisa would perform the same simple star lift in unison. He pressed Bailey up and rotated as she balanced her hip on his hand. When he swooped her down, she grinned.

"This is fun."

"It is," he agreed and meant it. He glanced at a skater who watched them avidly as they passed. "I believe you have an admirer, Bailey."

She followed his gaze and groaned good-naturedly. "Hi, Andrew!" She waved.

Poor Andrew Quinn blushed to the roots of his light hair and spun around to skate off in the other direction. As they met Dev and Kisa in the middle of the ice, Dev waggled his eyebrows.

"You know, B…he got his braces off."

She rolled her eyes. "He's still a teenager."

"You could do a lot worse. You have, in fact," Dev teased. "He was asking me if we're coming to Nationals in January. He was really excited to hear that Sue invited us to be official ambassadors."

"He's a great kid. Maybe I'll consider it in a few years once he's able to grow facial hair. Speaking of Sue, did you see she's here with some of the other Feds?"

Dev nodded. "We'll have to go play nice after practice."

Misha followed their gaze, tensing. Would the American federation try again to convince Dev and Bailey to return to competition?

Kisa motioned to a young girl at the other end of the ice. "They are very watchful of her."

The girl was barely five feet tall and skinny as a rail, with jet-black hair. She wore a pink leotard and spun in a blur, pulling her leg up behind her and holding it over her head with both hands in a Biellmann spin.

"Sabrina Pang, the next great hope," Bailey said. She pointed to the woman sitting in the stands watching Sabrina intently. "Her mom is intense. She skated for China back in the day but never made it. She was staring daggers at Hanako earlier. I wouldn't be surprised if she's got a Hanako voodoo doll in her purse. Sabrina's at our old training center in Colorado Springs. You remember our coach, Louise? She thinks it's going to get ugly when Sabrina starts growing. She's fourteen now, and you know how it is when girls get hips and boobs."

Kisa shuddered. "The jumps that were so easy suddenly feel impossible. Like you must relearn everything. It was a terrible time."

"Yep. And with a skating mom second guessing her coach at every turn, poor Sabrina's going to be under a hell of a lot of pressure. She seems like a nice kid. I hope she makes it."

"It is easier, being a man," Misha noted.

Kisa smirked. "You are just now realizing this?"

"Understatement of the millennium, Reznikov. Next you'll tell us water's wet," Bailey teased.

Laughing, Misha skated to Dev's side. "Dev, you will give me backup? Do not let them band together against me."

Dev slung his arm over Misha's shoulders. "Don't worry, I'll protect you. Back off, ladies." A moment later, his smile vanished and he dropped his arm. He glanced around the arena nervously. "We should get back to rehearsing. Kisa, you ready to go again?"

They skated off, and Misha couldn't help but feel as though he'd been slapped as he watched them go.

Bailey took his hand. "Hey, you okay? He didn't mean to..." She lowered her voice. "You want to keep it a secret too, right?"

He nodded, although he wasn't sure he believed it.

"Because I know he worries that we won't get as many shows if he comes out and we'll lose the few endorsements we have, but I've told him that if it's a choice between our pro career and his happiness, I will always pick door number two. Besides, maybe people will surprise us. If more skaters would just come out already, it wouldn't be such a big deal. I don't think the audience cares. I really don't."

"But there is much money at stake. I need to think of Kisa, just as Dev thinks of you."

Bailey shook her head. "If they don't want us to do Stars on Ice next year because you guys are gay, then screw them. Kisa agrees with me. We talked about it in great detail over many adult beverages." She sighed. "Look, you know we just want you and Dev to be happy, and we support whatever you guys want to do. But don't make yourselves miserable trying to protect us or some shit like that. Okay?"

What else could he say? "Okay. But it is for the best right now, I think. It will keep everything simple. Come, let us lift again."

As they stroked down the rink, gathering speed, Misha wasn't so sure simple was the right word at all.

Chapter Fourteen

★★★ ★★★

WHEN MISHA AND Kisa arrived for the interview the next night, Dev and Bailey were already waiting side by side on a plush gray love seat in the hotel lobby. A Christmas tree towered nearby, and carols filled the air. Sparkling garlands and decorations festooned the reception desk.

Two of NBC's publicists sat nearby to monitor the questions. The interviewer, a middle-aged woman, stood from her armchair and extended her hand.

"Barbara Fettle from the *Boston Globe*. A pleasure to meet you both." She indicated another love seat next to Dev and Bailey's. "Please make yourselves comfortable. I suppose no introductions are needed here."

They all chuckled amiably, and Misha wished he could be anywhere else. But he still had to play his part. He tried to get comfortable. Kisa had insisted he wear trousers and leather shoes along with his blue sweater as opposed to his usual jeans and sneakers. Oh how he missed his flip-flops. He glanced at Dev, who kept his gaze firmly on the interviewer.

Barbara sat in the armchair facing both teams and turned on her recorder. "You've all finished your competitive skating careers. What's retirement been like for you?"

As Dev spoke of his new foray into part-time coaching, Misha examined the floral arrangement on the table beside Barbara. It had been another long day of practice for the show—another long day of pretending. He and Dev had initially agreed not to risk being together at night since they were only in Boston for a week. They thought surely they could go without being intimate.

But Misha felt adrift and unsettled, as though he was starving for Dev's touch. It had only been days, but he longed to hold Dev and be held by him. To see him smile and hear him moan. To simply be near him. Dev had whispered earlier that he couldn't wait until they were home again in LA, and Misha had whole-heartedly agreed. They would meet in Misha's room as soon as they could escape the interview.

When he watched Dev, Bailey said he had hearts in his eyes, and Kisa agreed. They said the same of Dev, which had made Misha's stomach flutter foolishly. Even now, he smiled to himself.

As much as he loved seeing Kisa again, he longed to be home with Dev. Bickering in the kitchen over borscht or in the bathroom over the toothpaste. Or on the beach, racing each other across the sand with Zoloto at their heels. In the bedroom, bodies sweaty and tangled, fucking raw, tasting and touching and—

"Mikhail?"

As Kisa elbowed him, Misha glanced up to find all eyes on him. He smiled. "Apologies. Please repeat the question?"

Barbara smiled. "Of course. I was just noting that you're living in the Los Angeles area as well now, aren't you?" She tilted her head with a smile. "Do you and Dev ever run into each other?"

Misha kept his expression even. "Not yet." His tongue grew heavy with the lies.

"And how do you all feel performing together? You were quite the rivals for a few years. Is it a challenge to just turn off that competitiveness?"

Bailey spoke up. "Well, we're all athletes, so I don't think we can ever turn it off completely. But this show is all about family and the holidays, and we're part of the skating family."

"There are no hard feelings? Dev and Bailey, you were gunning for that gold in Annecy, and it must have been difficult to come so close."

The strain that filled the air was sudden but powerful. Misha had been so glad to let all this go, and he cursed this woman for mentioning it, even though he knew she was simply doing her job.

"Of course it was disappointing for us," Dev said. "But that's sports, and we certainly don't begrudge Kisa and Mikhail their hard-fought victory."

"And they won the World title here after the Olympics," Misha added. "We did not compete, and the gold was theirs. We were glad to give them the chance to win."

Barbara's eyebrows shot up. "Dev and Bailey? Any response? Did you feel your World title was earned? Or was it a gift from your absent Russian competitors?"

Wait, wait. Misha's heart plummeted. "I did not mean—"

"Of course we feel we earned it," Bailey said, her tone clipped. "While we performed very well in Annecy, at Worlds we had the two very best skates of our lives. We didn't put a foot wrong, and becoming world champions here in Dev's hometown was the highlight of our careers." Her hand was tight on Dev's arm, and Dev was smiling in a way that appeared painful. "And it's a thrill for us to be skating again in Boston on Christmas Eve for this incredible live event."

Kisa was frozen beside Misha. When he opened his mouth again, she gave him a withering look, and he sat back. The two publicists glared but relaxed when Barbara moved on to questions about the show. They gave the answers NBC wanted them to give, and Misha willed the interview to end as he rolled the damning words he had mistakenly said over in his mind again and again, wishing he could take them back.

When the interview finally did end, Kisa's phone buzzed, and she disappeared toward the elevators after giving him a squeeze.

Bailey, arms crossed over her chest, gave Misha a tight smile. "Later." Then she shared a glance with Dev and rolled her eyes.

Yes, clearly she was unhappy. As she left, Misha turned to Dev, who raised his hand.

"Just don't say anything else right now, okay? I need to…" His nostrils flared, and he glanced at Barbara and the publicists, who were now strolling toward the exit. "I don't know. I need to not talk to you right now."

"But—"

In a swirl of giggles, Caroline and Hanako entered the lobby. Misha instinctively stepped back from Dev, who turned on his heel and stalked toward the bank of elevators. Misha followed, smiling absently to the girls as they passed by on their way to the street. One of the elevators was closing, but he stuck his hand inside and the doors obediently bounced open.

Jaw tight, Dev kept his eyes straight forward. The older couple sharing the elevator with them were having a loud conversation about a duck and a boat, and Misha wished they would shut up.

Two buttons were illuminated—the eighth and the fifteenth floors. Misha's own anger began to simmer. Had they not decided Dev would stay with him tonight, despite the risk? Should they not even discuss it? Misha jabbed the button for his floor, the seventeenth.

The seconds stretched out as they traveled up. When the doors closed behind the couple, Misha turned to Dev. "Why have I upset you?"

"Why?" Dev asked incredulously. "If you don't know, then I don't know where to begin. No, wait, I do. How about you were being a pompous dick?"

Misha gritted his teeth. "I did not intend any offense. You know that."

"You acted like you did us a favor by not going to Worlds! Like we only won because you *gave* it to us! We skated our career best there! We could have beaten you fair and square! We worked *so* hard after Annecy to be the best we'd ever been, and we *were*. We did it. Not you giving us charity."

With a *ding*, the doors slid open. Shaking his head, Dev stepped off, but Misha tugged him back onto the elevator.

"Let me speak before you turn your back on me!"

Dev's eyes blazed. "Fine! What do you have to say?"

"First I would say that you're being like a child!"

"And you're being an arrogant asshole. Just like old times!"

They stared at each other for a long moment, breathing shallowly, and then Misha was stumbling back against the wall with Dev's weight against him. Dev gripped his sweater as they kissed ferociously, Misha tangling his fingers in Dev's hair roughly. They hadn't truly argued in so long, and his mind spun as frustration and desire clashed.

He was vaguely aware of the elevator doors opening and closing but couldn't tear himself away from Dev, who jammed his thigh between Misha's as they fought with their tongues. He couldn't get enough—the taste of Dev's mouth and his commanding touch, the feel of his powerful body. His anger evaporated. He'd get on his knees and beg forgiveness if it meant making things right between them.

But before he could, Dev tore himself away. "Jesus, we can't..." He shook his head and wiped his mouth. The elevator was now on the top floor, and Dev blindly stepped off.

Misha followed. The hallway was empty, and Dev pushed open a door that read *ROOF GARDEN ACCESS*. Of course the garden was long dead, with only empty trellises wobbling in the icy wind. Multi-colored Christmas lights ringed the roof, looped around the railing, and cast a soft glow. Neither of them wore coats, and Misha shoved his hands in his pockets. They stared at each other.

Dev's breath clouded the frigid air as he exhaled a long breath.

"What you said made me and Bailey feel like crap. Like our gold isn't real because you and Kisa let us have it by not competing. Look, you guys were the best. You still are. We know it. But having it thrown in our faces in front of a reporter sucked."

Remorse flooded Misha as he thought back to what he'd told the interviewer. Yes, he could see how his words sounded. "I did not intend for that, Vassenka. Please believe me." He took Dev's hand. "That was not my meaning. I am glad for your gold. It would sadden me greatly if you had never become world champion. It was deserved. If I could share Olympic gold with you, I would."

Dev's shoulders slumped. "I know. I know you would." He laced their fingers together. "Maybe we can dig up a judging scandal so they have to make it a tie. Those French judges are always shifty."

Misha smiled. "This is true." His smile faded. "I am very sorry for what I said. I think you and Bailey are beautiful skaters. You could be Russian, you are so graceful. You don't seem American on the ice at all."

Dev burst out laughing. "Okay, maybe you should just stop talking tonight. Your foot is apparently stuck in your mouth."

"My...what?" Misha frowned. "Ah yes. The foot in the mouth. But I only mean to compliment you!"

"Quit while you're ahead." Dev wrapped his arms around Misha's waist and kissed him softly. After a moment, he glanced around guiltily. "We should go inside. That was really stupid of us in the elevator. Anyone could have seen us."

Somehow Misha found he didn't care. He was *supposed* to care, but would it truly be so terrible? For how long could they go on hiding this way? "Maybe it would be all right."

"What about your family in Russia?"

"They are fine. I am not competing any longer. The officials have no say anymore. Perhaps I have been too cautious. Too scared."

"What about our careers? You know we won't be asked to do as many shows."

"I do not need their shows."

Dev tensed. "You may not, but I do. I love skating. I'm not ready to give it up." He stepped back, shaking his head. "Not yet. I can't."

"I know, I know." Misha drew him near again and kissed him lightly. "I know. It's all right. It's our secret."

"Okay," Dev whispered, still stiff.

Misha tried to lighten the mood. "Who knows? Perhaps it will make us more popular. They will want us to skate together."

Dev laughed softly. "Like *Blades of Glory?* Yeah, that'll go down really well. You're taller, so I guess you'll have to lift me."

"Not a problem." Misha bent his knees and wrapped his arms around Dev's hips before hoisting him off the ground with a grunt. "You will need to go on diet after all. Kisa will give you tips." He spun around.

Head back, Dev threw his arms out. "We'll revolutionize the sport!"

He was beautiful in the night, and Misha wanted to kiss his long throat. Laughing, they stumbled around until Misha had to put Dev down or risk straining his back. He knew they should talk further, but they smiled so easily as they went back inside.

There would be another day for talking.

In Misha's room with the door locked and a low lamp lit, he kissed Dev again. "You forgive me, yes?"

"Yes. I'm sorry I got angry."

"I was very bad with what I said. I'm sorry."

"I know." Dev leaned their foreheads together. "It's okay. We're all bad sometimes."

The current of desire that was ever present when Dev was around flared. He took Dev's earlobe between his teeth. "Perhaps I should be punished," he whispered.

Dev inhaled sharply and pulled back to take Misha's face in his hands. "You want that?"

"Da. What shall you do to me?" Misha's whole body tingled.

Dev hesitated, his eyes searching. "What do you want me to do to you?"

Excitement raced in Misha's veins as Dev ran his calloused thumb over Misha's bottom lip. He blurted out the words before he lost his nerve. "Take me over your knee."

Eyes going darker, Dev took a shuddering breath and stepped back. "Take off your clothes."

Misha did as he was told, and Dev slowly sat on the edge of the bed. He was still fully dressed in his jeans and green sweater, and he spread his legs, watching avidly as Misha stripped down. After the cold of the roof, Misha felt aflame, his skin flushed and his cock growing without being touched. When he was naked, he stood waiting.

"You're so beautiful," Dev murmured. He cleared his throat. "Now come here," he commanded.

Misha took the few steps to the bed. Again he waited while Dev drank him in with his eyes. He wanted to reach out and touch, to kiss and run his hands through Dev's thick hair and tell him he was the most beautiful man Misha had ever known. But he stayed silent and played his role, anticipation making his head light.

With the barest touch of his fingertips, Dev traced Misha's dick from base to tip. Misha swallowed thickly. He wanted to beg Dev to take him in his mouth, but of course Dev didn't. He concentrated on breathing as Dev lightly explored his cock and balls as though there was nothing but time. Being on display made Misha's breath stutter in his throat, need building deep in his belly. The featherlight touches had him trembling.

Without warning, Dev yanked him over his lap. Misha flailed

for a moment, heart racing as he fought for balance, bracing himself with his hands on the floor. He was too tall to be anything resembling graceful in this position, but he settled onto Dev's thighs with his ass in the air and his head hanging down.

He bent his legs and tried to relax. The denim of Dev's jeans was rough against Misha's groin, and he rubbed against it for a moment of delicious friction.

He waited.

The only sound in the room was their harsh breathing. Misha yearned for the smack of Dev's hand, while fearing it a little too. But there was nothing. He stared at the carpet—gray squares repeated in geometric patterns. Finally, when he thought he might scream for something—*anything*—to happen, Dev's fingers dipped into the crease of Misha's ass, and Misha held his breath.

As he had with Misha's cock and balls, Dev explored with only feathery touches, barely skimming Misha's sensitive flesh until Misha was squirming and arching his ass up, desperate. Dev's thickening cock nudged Misha's hip, and Misha was hard against Dev's thighs. He wanted to squeeze his hand between them and jerk himself, but he resisted.

When Dev parted Misha's ass cheeks and pressed around the rim of his hole, Misha moaned. "*Spasibo. Spasibo.* Please, Vassenka."

He felt wetness and looked over his shoulder to find Dev spitting onto him. Dev's gaze was riveted as he rubbed his saliva around Misha's hole. When he inched his finger inside, Misha wanted to cry with relief. He grasped at it, wanting more. He closed his eyes and hung his head again.

"So greedy. So perfect," Dev muttered.

Then his hand swatted down on Misha's ass cheek. Misha cried out, even though it was too soft. "Da. More."

The first few strikes were tentative, but as Misha gasped and ground his hardness against Dev, the smacks became more certain.

Alternating one cheek and then the other, Dev spanked him hard, the sounds echoing in the room. Misha's ass began to sting, and it was *wonderful*. He'd never played with a lover like this—he'd had so few and had been young—but he was completely confident Dev would never truly hurt him. His flesh felt hot, and he panted with his mouth open, wanting more and less at the same time.

The sweet torment continued, with Dev stopping at times to caress Misha's burning skin and tease his hole. Then it would start again, and Misha was caught between pleasure and pain, and his heart raced at the thrill of it.

Cock leaking now, he was on fire, the smacks in the air spurring him on as he neared the edge. Draped over Dev, he felt totally exposed and bare. *Free.* He squirmed as the pain become searing, and Dev held him in place with his other hand heavy on Misha's back. Misha opened his eyes and twisted his neck to catch sight of Dev's intense expression. Dev's lips were parted, his eyes piercing.

"You can't come until I tell you." Dev's voice was firm.

Misha could only whimper and submit as Dev slapped the backs of Misha's upper thighs. He hung his head again and thought he might explode and come anyway, but then the pleasure and anticipation seemed to go even deeper, and he shivered, eager for more. His ass was raw, and he cried out with each strike as Dev moved back to his cheeks. Sweat dripped into his eyes, and his arms and legs shook.

Suddenly Dev was hauling him up and Misha was on his knees between Dev's legs. Dev's hands were steady on his shoulders. "Let me see you come."

Misha barely touched himself before he was shooting, splattering the bedspread that hung down over the end of the bed. The wave of his orgasm rushed through him, and the pleasure was so intense he had to close his eyes, his head back and mouth open. He would have toppled over if not for Dev's strong, safe grasp.

He wavered as Dev moved, still not opening his eyes as Dev bent him over the mattress. Chest heaving, Misha pressed his cheek to the duvet, warm from where Dev had sat. He could hear Dev swearing under his breath, along with the sound of a zipper. Then Dev's cock was against him, and Misha braced himself for a rough fuck.

But Dev only slid his cock into the crease of Misha's ass. Grunting, he slid up and down, his sweater harsh against Misha's tender flesh. With only a few thrusts, he was coming, splashing Misha's ass. Dev groaned and dropped his head to Misha's back. His breath was hot.

"Oh my God. You're amazing. Have I mentioned that before? Because you are."

Misha wanted to answer but couldn't summon the will.

With gentle hands, Dev lifted Misha's hips and helped him climb onto the bed far enough to flop down on his stomach. Dev collapsed beside him on his side, still dressed except for his jeans and underwear pulled down to his hips, his softening dick hanging out. Dev smoothed his palm over Misha's back.

"Okay?"

Misha found the energy to smile. "Da. Very good, in fact."

"I didn't hurt you? I mean, not too much? I mean, not in a good way?" Dev's brow furrowed and he grazed his hand over Misha's tender skin. "You're really red."

"It was perfect."

Dev propped himself up on his elbow and bent to inspect Misha's ass. "Are you sure?"

"I am sure. I would say otherwise."

"Okay." For a moment, Dev appeared flustered, and he smiled awkwardly. "I've never done anything like that before."

"Neither have I." Misha lifted his hand and brushed back Dev's curls. "But I liked it. I think you did too?"

"Oh yeah. I liked it."

Dev grinned his beautiful smile that made Misha's stomach flip-flop, and Misha drew him down for a lazy kiss. "Then we are in agreement."

"We are." Dev snuggled in close. "We should get cleaned up."

"Hmm. In a minute." Misha shifted. The burning in his skin was fading, being replaced by a tingly soreness that pleased him. "I hope I will not fall tomorrow. Perhaps we should not do this when we are to skate."

Dev laughed. "Good call." He pushed himself up and leaned over Misha's ass again. "Don't worry. I'll kiss it better."

Misha shut his eyes as he felt the careful softness of Dev's lips against his tender skin. He moaned in disappointment when Dev raised his head.

"But next time we should have a safe word. Just in case it goes too far. Do you know what I mean?"

Misha peered over his shoulder. "Like a codeword to stop. Our little secret, yes?"

Dev smiled tenderly. "Da." He bent his head to kiss Misha's ass again.

Humming, Misha closed his eyes. This secret he would be delighted to keep close to his heart.

Chapter Fifteen

"ORCHIDS—MY FAVORITE." BAILEY touched a delicate purple petal and cradled the bouquet in her arm. "But of course you knew that. Thanks, Misha." She went up on tiptoes and pressed a kiss to his cheek. She waved him into her hotel room and shut the door behind him. "Let me just put these in water."

"I hope you will forgive my thoughtlessness." He played with the zipper pull on his hoodie. It would affect his relationship with Dev if Bailey was angry with him, but more than that, Misha found himself genuinely contrite. He liked Bailey and did not want to upset her.

As she squeezed the flowers into a glass of water in the bathroom, Bailey called back, "Apology accepted." She plucked her purse from the bed. "We all have our moments. Is everything cool with you and Dev?"

A flicker of excitement went through him. "Yes."

Her eyebrow lifted sky high. "Oh, I see. You guys made up but good, huh? You're practically *glowing*."

He didn't bother denying it and only smiled slyly.

"I love it." She grinned. "Okay, we'd better hit the road."

Misha opened the door as Bailey mumbled something about lip gloss and hustled back to the bathroom. He turned, blinking at the slight blonde in the doorway with her fist raised. "Caroline."

She blinked back. "Mikhail! I'm sorry, I must have the wrong room." Her eyes widened as she peered around him.

Bailey was there at his shoulder. "Sweet! Hey. I was just coming to meet you in the lobby."

"Sorry. I wanted to borrow your team jacket because stupid Grant spilled tomato juice all over mine at breakfast this morning. He and I have a photo thing this morning with this reporter from Buffalo." She glanced at Misha. "That's where Grant's from. Buffalo. It's in New York. State, I mean. Obviously. But you probably need yours, Bailey, so I can just get it dry cleaned or we won't wear our jackets in the pictures, which would be fine. Totally fine."

Still a teenager, Caroline rambled the way she always did in Misha's presence. He wasn't sure if it was him or just her normal state of being—flustered and uncertain.

"It's no problem. Let me just grab it," Bailey said.

Misha and Caroline smiled awkwardly at each other. Misha cleared his throat. "I was just here to…" His mind was frustratingly blank.

"It's cool! None of my business. I shouldn't have just shown up unannounced."

Bailey reappeared and thrust the blue jacket with red-and-white adornments at Caroline. "Here you go, Sweet. Mikhail and I were just going to meet Dev and Kisa. We've got another joint interview thing later, so we're going over our answers."

"Oh, right. Of course." Caroline nodded rapidly. "Okay, bye!" She scurried away and disappeared around the corner toward the elevators.

Bailey sighed. "Terrific."

"She thinks that we are…" He motioned between them.

"Yep."

"She will speak to others?"

With a snort, Bailey closed her door. "This is figure skating.

Gossip is like, our fifth and most important food group. Her thumbs are undoubtedly tapping out tales of our scandalous hook-up as we speak." She linked her hand through his arm. "On the bright side, no one will suspect a thing about you and Dev."

A FROWN CREASED Kisa's face as she and Misha stroked around the rink. "Has something happened? Why do they whisper?"

Bailey had been right, of course, and it was clear the rumor of their supposed affair had spread through the cast as if Caroline had set a match to fireworks. Andrew glared at him as he skated by, and Misha sighed. "They think Bailey and I are a couple."

Kisa laughed. "Close, but not quite. Why in heaven would they think that?"

As Misha filled her in, she laughed even harder.

He huffed. "It is not funny! Look at how Andrew stares at me. I do not want to be a villain."

"Misha, we have been the villains for years. Pay them no mind."

Dev and Bailey were taking a break at one end of the rink, leaning by the boards and eating bananas. Misha willed Dev to look up as he neared, but to no avail.

"Kisa and Mikhail?" One of the PAs called out. "It's your turn to practice your solo."

Most of the other skaters hung out in the stands, snacking and chatting, while Dev and Bailey were still in the far corner. Misha turned away, tugged off his black warm-up jacket, and straightened his gray T-shirt. *Time to concentrate.* He and Kisa took their opening position, holding each other's hands and staring lovingly into each other's eyes. As the music began, Misha took a deep breath. It was "Time After Time," an old song Kisa had loved since, as a child, her mother had secretly listened to it on pirate radio. It was perfect for an exhibition—stirring and romantic and nostalgic for many people in the audience.

In exhibitions, they never did side-by-side jumps, and neither did most pair teams. Too much risk, since a fall in an exhibition could ruin it. Later there would be a throw triple toe since Kisa could land those in her sleep, and their first big trick was their split triple twist—one of their very best elements.

They rounded the rink with crossovers as the music built to the chorus, and he gripped Kisa's waist, both of them skating backwards. As Kisa used her toe pick to spring up, Misha turned, skidding a little with his left blade to open up his body and vault her above his head, watching her rotate through the air in a blur and reaching up to—

Everything went black as pain exploded below his eye. He grappled blindly for Kisa as he lost his balance and crashed back onto the ice, the breath knocked from him like a punch. Kisa sprawled on top of him, and he blinked, trying to clear his vision. For a moment he could only see bright lights before Kisa's stricken face swam above him. She was saying something, but he couldn't understand what.

Then, as if he had removed ear plugs, sound returned. He could hear the panicked shouts of the PAs and producers calling for the medics, and Kisa knelt at his side, touching his face gently. Then Dev appeared on his other side, eyes wild.

"Misha!" Dev touched his head and body, as if prodding for injuries. "Can you hear me?"

"Of course." Misha tried to sit up, but Dev and Kisa held him down.

Bailey hovered behind Dev, her face pinched.

"No. You might have hit your head when you fell," Dev said. He brushed back Misha's hair. "It's okay. You're going to be okay." He took Misha's hand. "Does it hurt? Of course it hurts; you just got an elbow in the face."

Tears slipped down Kisa's cheeks. "It was my fault. I didn't pick in hard enough. I was too low."

"Shh." Misha patted her. "I am fine. Truly. I can get up." His cheek throbbed and he would likely have bruises on his back, but he was sure he had kept his head up when he fell. Although there was so much pain throbbing through him, he couldn't be positive.

"No!" Dev kept his hand on Misha's chest. "Just wait." He yelled over his shoulder. "Seriously, where are the medics?" He kissed Misha's forehead. "Just don't move until they check you over."

Near Misha's feet, Caroline and Hanako stood, watching with matching head tilts and baffled expressions. Andrew and Grant looked at each other and then back at Misha and Dev.

Grant cleared his throat. "Um...what's happening? Are you guys..."

"Yes, they're fucking!" Bailey announced. She leaned over Dev's shoulder. "How are you doing, Misha? Hanging in there?"

"Fine. Let me up." He tried to move, but Kisa and Dev were unrelenting.

"But I thought..." Caroline trailed off. "*Dev* and *Mikhail?* Wait, Mikhail's *gay?*"

In unison, Bailey, Dev, and Kisa answered, "Yes!"

Misha laughed, grimacing as his back spasmed. The medics shoved through the assembled group and ordered Kisa and Dev out of the way. They poked Misha and shone light in his eyes, asking him questions and insisting on a neck brace and backboard. When Misha protested, one of the producers stepped in.

"It's a liability issue. We're transporting you to the hospital for tests. No argument."

"But..." With a grumble, he gave in.

"Kisa and I are riding with him," Dev told the producer firmly.

The rest of the skaters still stood nearby, looking back and forth between Misha and Dev with varying degrees of astonishment as Misha was loaded onto a stretcher.

Bailey rolled her eyes. "For the record, you guys are all, like, totally blind. And once you get over the shock, they're pretty freaking adorable. So get over it already." She gave Misha's arm a squeeze. "Good thing you've got a hard head, right?"

"Very solid," Misha agreed.

Then they were wheeling him off the ice and through the back of the arena. He could only see the vast ceiling above him, pipes crisscrossing through the concrete. He caught glimpses of the head of one of the paramedics, and his chest tightened, although he was sure Dev and Kisa were close behind. He relaxed a bit as he heard clomping that had to be them running to catch up in their skate guards.

Snow landed wet on his face as he was rolled outside and maneuvered around into a waiting ambulance.

"Sorry, only one person can ride with him," a paramedic said nearby, his voice sounding too loud to Misha's ears. He could only clearly see the roof of the ambulance with his head immobilized, and he tried to look down at where Dev perched by his other side, Kisa on the steps.

Kisa's eyes glistened. "I will go in taxi."

"No, you're coming with us." Dev tugged her onto his lap, glaring at the paramedic. "It's fine; we both fit."

Misha couldn't see the paramedic, but after a moment, the man sighed. "Okay, okay, but only since the hospital is close."

As the siren wailed and they sped away, the paramedic took his vitals, his pen scratching paper near Misha's head.

Dev leaned over and smiled shakily. "Bailey's right. You'll be fine."

"Please, do not worry."

"Of course we worry." Kisa clutched his thigh. "You will have all the tests." She addressed the paramedic. "Do you think any bones are broken?"

Gently, the paramedic probed Misha's cheek. "I don't think so."

"How is your elbow?" Misha asked.

"Sore." Kisa smiled tremulously. "You do have a very hard head."

Dev still watched him anxiously, and Misha took his cold, sweaty hand. "Do not worry so much, Vassenka."

"There are just so many things—" Dev blew out a breath. "Are we almost there?" he asked the paramedic.

"Less than a minute out. But really, I think he's fine. No signs of head trauma."

"Okay." Dev nodded. "Okay. You're going to be fine, Misha."

"This is what I tell you."

Dev kissed him softly. "And you're always right."

"I would not say always," Kisa muttered.

"Good point," Dev replied.

"Wait, wait, now you gang up. It is unfair." Misha winced as he tried to smile, the ambulance slowing.

When they took him away for the tests, although his body was sore, his heart sang.

"OKAY, NOW SIT down." Dev gently guided Misha to the side of the bed and knelt at his feet, going to work on the laces of his sneakers.

"I can take off my own shoes!" Misha laughed. "I am barely injured. I'm fine, Vassenka."

"Just because you don't have a concussion doesn't mean you aren't hurt. You hit the ice hard." Dev pulled off Misha's shoes and socks and then stood. "Arms up."

Misha did as he was told, and Dev pulled off his T-shirt. "Are you going to bathe me once you have removed all my clothes?" He leered. "I would enjoy that."

"This isn't funny!" Dev ran a hand through his tousled hair. "God, Misha. I can't…" He exhaled sharply.

Blinking, Misha reached for him, but Dev paced to the bathroom and then back again.

"I am fine. It's only a bruise." He touched his swollen and tender cheek. Fortunately Kisa's elbow had missed his eye and hadn't broken his cheekbone. The slight bruises on his back were nothing. "Why are you so serious?"

"Because you scared the hell out of me! You know what kind of head injuries can happen when a twist comes down wrong like that. I heard the gasp from everyone, and I was all the way down the rink when I saw you go down. I was so scared. In that moment it was like I could see everything we haven't done yet. Everything we would lose if something happened to you. Everything I would lose if I didn't have you."

Still sitting on the side of the bed, Misha tried to think of the right words. He wanted to go to him, but Dev seemed as though he was coming out of his skin. "I am here. You have lost nothing. Do not be afraid."

"But I am." Dev took a deep breath and blew it out as he started to pace back and forth on the gray carpet. "I'm afraid. That's why I haven't told my parents about you. Why I didn't want anyone to know. It's been so good—moving in together, finding a new job and learning how to coach. Being with you…it's been perfect. I keep waiting for the other shoe to drop."

Misha frowned. "A shoe?"

"Sorry, it's a saying. It means I'm waiting for something to go wrong when everything's right. Because it seems impossible that things would be this good. And I love my parents and my family, but…I honestly don't know how they'll feel about us being together. I don't want anyone to ruin this. I want to keep you all to myself in our little bubble. I want to keep you safe."

Wordlessly, Misha held out his hand. Dev closed the distance between them and took it, dropping to his knees by Misha's feet. Misha caressed Dev's hair as their eyes met. "I wish the same for you. I have my own fears."

"We'll figure it out." Dev rubbed his hands lightly up and down Misha's thighs. "Right?"

"Right." Misha fervently hoped it was true.

When Dev held him, Misha couldn't stop himself from wincing, and Dev immediately sat back.

"Shit. Sorry." He stood and nudged Misha back. "Lie down. You need to rest."

Misha did as he was told and let Dev remove the rest of his clothes. When Dev left Misha's boxer briefs, Misha huffed and peeled them off himself. "Come. I am not mortally wounded. I want to feel you against me."

Dev shook his head. "You need to rest."

"Yes, with you close. Clothes off."

"Aren't you bossy today?" But Dev was already kicking off his jeans and underwear with a little smile.

Misha grinned. "Perhaps I will command you tonight." He watched Dev strip off the rest of his clothes.

"At your service." Dev stood by the bed, the low light in the room shadowing the contours of his lean muscles. He lowered his voice. "What do you want me to do?"

"Come closer." He urged Dev closer until he straddled Misha's hips. For a moment, Misha simply drank in the sight of him—dark hair scattered on his broad chest and down his belly to his thick cock—already curving slightly upward. A smile played on Dev's full lips, his eyes bright with anticipation. Misha rested his hands on Dev's powerful thighs. "Pleasure yourself."

Dev didn't hesitate to take his cock in hand and begin stroking it. "Like this?"

"Da. Get hard for me."

It didn't take long. Lips parted, Dev worked his shaft, easing back his foreskin and jerking himself until the head was flushed and glistening. Misha swiped a drop with his fingertip and tasted it, making Dev groan, his muscles flexing as he brought himself closer to the edge. Sweat glistened in the hollow of his throat.

"*Tak krasivo.* You are so beautiful like this," Misha murmured, rubbing Dev's legs.

"So are you. Fuck, yes." He gasped and stroked himself faster, his other hand stealing down to caress his balls.

"Touch your nipples. Squeeze the way you like me to do."

Swallowing hard, Dev lifted his hand to flick and tease until his nipples were erect, still moving his hand on his cock harder and faster. "Jesus, Misha. I'm going to come soon. Do you want me in you?"

He thought of the first night in Tokyo. "Come all over me."

With a cry, Dev did just that, eyes open as he shuddered and milked himself, splattering Misha's stomach and chest. "Oh fuck," he muttered. He leaned a hand on Misha's shoulder as he caught his breath. "Fuck," he repeated.

Misha's pulse thundered, and he was hard just from watching. "Feed it to me."

Dev's eyes widened, and he quickly swiped his finger across Misha's chest and held it up. Slowly, Misha sucked Dev's finger between his lips, swirling around it with his tongue and savoring the salty musk. He let Dev's finger go with a wet *pop.* "Each drop."

Dev eagerly complied, moaning softly as Misha licked his finger clean again and again. When there was no more, Dev waited, breathing shallowly. "What do you want me to do now?"

"*Sosi menya.*" At Dev's furrowed brow, he translated. "Suck me."

As if he were in a race, Dev scooted back and bent to swallow

Misha's leaking cock. He sucked the head, his tongue tracing around it and up and down the ridge on the underside while he twisted his hand around the base. Dev's cheeks hollowed as he sucked harder.

"Fuck, fuck, fuck," Misha muttered. "*Moy khoroshiy.*" Dev looked up at him beneath his lashes, and Misha ran his palm over Dev's hair. "My good one. Make me come."

With a sly smile, Dev lifted his head and sucked his index finger before taking Misha's cock in his mouth again. Misha lifted his hips as Dev slipped his hand underneath and found his hole. He inched in, finding just the right angle to make Misha jerk off the bed, his balls tightening and his release ripping through him as Dev sucked him deeply.

He shivered as Dev coaxed him with his finger, tongue, and lips, not stopping until Misha reached for him. "Enough."

Gingerly, Dev stretched out beside him, kissing him softly. "How do you feel?"

"Not made of glass, Vassenka." He tugged Dev closer with a smile, closing his eyes as sleep rushed to take him. "That was the best kind of medicine."

Chapter Sixteen

"**I** HAVE IMPORTANT news, Misha." Papa's voice fairly vibrated over the crackling phone line, the Russian words quick and urgent.

Misha's breath caught, and he bolted up in bed, wide awake, wincing at the sudden movement. "Yes? Has something happened? Is everyone all right? Mama? Elena?"

"Yes, yes. This is good news."

With a long exhale, Misha sagged back against his pillows. After the final rehearsal that afternoon, he'd returned to his room for a shower and nap. Dev had more interviews to do, so Misha was alone. "You frightened me. What has happened?"

"We have had the local elections. Many new candidates have succeeded. Not only here in St. Petersburg, but across the country. Things are changing, Misha. The people are being heard. I know the leaders in Moscow will not go without a fight, but for the first time in years, we have much hope."

Misha's heart soared. "Do you think they will change the laws?"

"We can hope. More and more people are speaking out. The church is losing some of its influence. It feels as though we are moving forward again."

For a moment, Misha couldn't speak through the thickness in his throat. "Maybe I can stop hiding."

"I pray for this."

Misha had to take a shuddering breath, tears suddenly in his eyes.

"Now you are frightening me, Misha. This was to be happy news. Is something wrong?"

His chest was unbearably tight, and for a moment Misha thought perhaps the accident had done more damage than they thought. But then the sob broke through, although he tried to contain it.

As the tears flowed down his cheeks, he gripped his cell phone, heaving great breaths while his father patiently murmured words of comfort as he did so long ago when Misha suffered any sorrow as a boy.

Sniffling loudly, Misha swiped his arm over his face. "I'm sorry, Papa."

"Tell me what it is."

"I thought..." Misha sniffed again and took a deep breath. "I thought I could live happily in secret. That as long as I could find my little place by the ocean, I would be free and content. That as long as I had Dev, even if we had to hide away, I wouldn't care."

"But you do care."

He blew out another breath, more tears forming. "Yes, Papa. I do. I'm so happy when I'm with him, but we can't even go to the market together. To dinner or to ride the Ferris wheel. It is not a full life. But I worry about you and Mama and Elena and the children, and Kisa and her family, even though I am so far away now. I worry that there will still be some retribution for my rebellion. I couldn't live with myself, Papa."

His father's voice grew stern. "Misha, stop this way of thinking. No more of this, you hear me? We agreed you should stay away from home for the time being, but there is little danger to us. Especially now as the government loses power. We must be brave. We must stand up for what is right. For truth. Tell me right now—is this why you keep yourself hidden? For our benefit?"

"Not only, but yes. Papa, if they went after you—"

"Enough," he barked. "Misha, I am not afraid. You must live your life. Be free. You're Olympic champion. You are a hero of our people. Do not hide. The people need to hear the truth. In honesty, there is power."

Staring at the ceiling, Misha trembled all over. "Do you think so, Papa?"

"Yes."

"But it's not so easy. It's not just Russia. You know what it's like in skating. If everyone knew about me and Dev, we might not get the tours anymore. We have to think of Kisa and Bailey. We cannot be selfish."

"And have you asked them?"

"Well…"

"You know Kisa loves you above money. You know this."

"Yes." Bailey's words returned to him. *"…Don't make yourselves miserable trying to protect us or some shit like that."*

"If you are not bold, who will be?"

"But…" Misha thought of Dev, and his heart clenched. "Dev hasn't even told his parents about me."

"If he is ashamed of you—"

"No, no. He is not. But he's afraid."

"Then you must show how to be brave."

A soft knock at the door startled him, and Misha winced as he pushed himself up, his back twinging.

"Room service."

He'd forgotten he'd scheduled an early dinner to be delivered. "Papa, I must go."

"Think about what I've said. Promise me."

"Yes. I promise. Thank you, Papa. I love you. Tell Mama and Elena as well."

"All of our love is with you, Misha."

Misha hurried to the door and tipped the young man who delivered the meal. The grilled salmon and rice was entirely unappetizing at the moment, but as he forced himself to chew and swallow, his father's words echoed loudly in his mind.

"You must show how to be brave."

WHEN KISA OPENED her door, she exclaimed softly and reached for Misha's hand. "You have been crying."

They had to be downstairs for the shuttle to the arena in ten minutes, but Misha let her lead him inside, leaving his small suitcase by the door. "I hoped it wouldn't show."

"Are you in pain? We should not skate! I knew it was too much."

"No, no. It is not that."

"Then what has happened? My mother told me such good news today, about the elections. Did you not hear?" She rubbed his arms. "What's wrong?"

"Would you really not mind if it wasn't a secret anymore? About who I really am?"

Kisa's face softened. "Oh, Misha. Do you really have to ask? Of course not."

"Even if it means no more skating? You love it so much."

"I do. But yes, even if it means that. I don't think it will. I think people will surprise us. Even if they don't...I think you will feel better." She placed her hand against his chest. "You have always been heavy here, and I want you to fly the way I do on the ice."

Tears pricked his eyes again. "But what if, when you return home—"

"What?" Her eyes blazed. "What can they do? The people love us, Misha. *Our* people. Change is happening. I'm sure of it." She dashed away a tear from his cheek, tsking. "Come, let's fix you up." She nudged him toward the bed.

Misha sat on the end of it while Kisa unzipped her case and pulled out her huge makeup bag.

"First the drops. Look up."

He did as he was told, opening and closing his eyes as instructed as Kisa dabbed on makeup and brushed powder over his skin. When her room phone rang, she cursed and answered curtly that they'd be right down for the shuttle.

"They can wait a few minutes. We are Olympic champions, after all."

Misha smiled softly. "Yes. We are."

She brushed her fingertips across Misha's bruised cheek. "There. You can hardly see it, and your eyes are much less puffy." She kissed his forehead. "No more tears until after the show, yes?"

"Yes."

Kisa hesitated. "Have you told Dev how you really feel?"

The heaviness returned. "No."

"You know, I was not sure what to think at first. I honestly didn't think it would last beyond the summer. But I see he makes you very happy. He cares for you very much. He is a good man."

Misha swallowed hard. "Yes."

"At the hospital, he could not sit for even a moment. You are in his heart. And he is in yours, yes?"

Nodding, Misha pushed down a swell of emotion.

"Then you have to tell him the truth." She tugged his hand. "All right, time to go before they come looking."

He caught her hand, lifting it for a kiss.

Outside the hotel, the shuttle van waited with the other skaters inside. Kisa and Misha hurried, murmuring apologies, and took the empty seat at the front. When Misha glanced back to where Dev and Bailey sat a few rows behind, Dev was watching him with his brows pulled together, lines of concern on his face.

Misha wanted more than anything to go to him immediately and tell him how he was feeling, but instead he smiled in what he hoped was a reassuring way and then turned back around. The packed little bus was not the place, and he needed to refocus his mind on the show. He was being paid well by NBC, and it was important to perform his best. He had to put everything else aside and do his job.

In his pocket, his phone vibrated, and he pulled it out.

What's wrong? Are you okay?

Misha quickly tapped out a reply to Dev.

Only tired. Do not worry.

Dev's reply was almost immediate.

I'm still worried.

A smile tugged on Misha's lips, warmth in his chest.

It is your Christmas Eve. Be merry, Vassenka. All is well.

One of the PAs in the other front seat of the bus stood and cleared her throat. "We're almost there, so I just want to make sure everyone knows their schedule as we count down to show-time. Dev and Bailey, the local news is waiting to do a fluff piece with you, as well as Andrew, Grant, and Caroline." She consulted her clipboard. "Mikhail and Kisa, NBC's going to film a little spot explaining the accident in practice."

"Wait, you don't want the folks at home thinking he got into a bar fight?" Bailey asked.

The PA snorted. "Doesn't quite fit into our 'peace on Earth, goodwill to all men' vibe." She glanced at Misha. "Great job with the makeup, though. Still, with HD, that bruise will be clear as day."

Misha's phone shuddered.

I can't wait to be alone with you again.

He quickly responded with a few excited emoticons and a smile over his shoulder. He only hoped Dev would be as eager to see him once he heard what was weighing on Misha's mind.

"OF COURSE WE all remember the terrible collision in practice just before you were set to compete at the Olympic Games. Kisa, you were an inspiration to us all as you skated through that rib injury despite the pain."

Misha's stomach churned at the memory of the other skater slamming into Kisa and the bang she made when she spun into the boards.

"After that terrible accident, what did it mean to you to win that gold medal?"

As Kisa answered the reporter, Misha rolled his eyes in his mind, aware of course of the camera on them. He truly wished journalists would not ask such silly questions. What did it mean? Everything, of course.

The woman turned to him with dazzling teeth. "And here we are with Mikhail sporting the injury this time. Can you tell us what happened?"

He smiled. "It was nothing, really. Only a little accident on the triple twist. I am fine. We have bad luck, it seems."

"I have sharp elbows," Kisa added. "But he is very tough."

"I'd say you both are!" The woman chuckled. "Glad you're okay, Mikhail. We can't wait to see you guys skate tonight. What a way to ring in the holidays. Merry Christmas!"

They nodded and smiled, and then it was mercifully over. Misha hurried to the locker room, but Dev was already gone, or perhaps he hadn't made it yet. Misha changed into his first costume—a red silk shirt and green pants like all the other men wore for the opening number—and paced restlessly.

Andrew cleared his throat. "You doing okay? You seem a little on edge. Which is weird, because usually you're scarily calm."

Misha bit back the urge to snap at him, smiling tensely instead. "I always hid it well."

Grant laughed. "You sure did. You always hid a lot well."

"Dude," Andrew whispered.

Grant held up his hands, his red shirt half buttoned. "I didn't mean anything by it. It's cool. You and Dev? Totally cool. I just didn't see it coming, that's all."

"It is fine. Thank you." Misha escaped the locker room. If he couldn't see Dev, he needed air and quiet. He slipped away to one of the farthest corners of the backstage area to gather himself.

It was silly to be nervous. There would be no stern-faced judges watching his every move. No medals were on the line. He had skated in hundreds of shows and galas over the years, and this one should be no different.

Of course, he knew very well his nerves weren't about the show. As he walked down a hallway, his skate guards clacking on the cement, his father's words looped in his mind again.

"You must show how to be brave."

What if he asked too much of Dev? Coming out was not an easy thing, and he didn't want to apply pressure. He didn't want to make the wrong choice—the reckless choice—no matter what his father and Kisa insisted.

A woman's raised voice broke into his thoughts, and he peered around a corner. A short, plump Indian woman just inside a door argued with a security guard. She wore a sparkling gold blouse, large hoop earrings adorned her ears, and her shoulder-length dark hair was neatly coiffed. As she motioned with her hands, many bangles clanged together.

"Listen, I need to see my son. I have to give him something very important."

The young security guard shook his head. "I'm sorry, ma'am, but I can't let you backstage."

"My son is the star of this show! What, you think I'm some criminal? I only need to see him for a minute."

The guard shifted from foot to foot. "I wish I could help you, but I can't let anyone in before the show."

She harrumphed with a jangle. "Fine, young man. Then can you give him something for me?" She opened her purse.

"I can." Misha spoke before he could think better of it.

Mrs. Avira and the guard spun toward him, and Misha stepped out fully from behind the corner and walked toward them. His palms sweated, and he tried for a friendly smile, likely failing miserably. "I'll be seeing Dev in a moment."

For a few seconds, Mrs. Avira only blinked. Then she pasted on a smile. "If it's no trouble, that would be very nice of you."

"No trouble at all."

"Did somebody punch you?" She pointed at his face.

Misha huffed out a laugh. "No. Kisa and I had a little accident on the triple twist."

Mrs. Avira winced. "Ah yes. The elbow. Devassy had his share of black eyes, but never anything broken, thank the Lord."

Misha's mind whirled. There was so much he wanted to say, yet of course he couldn't utter a word of it. *What was Dev like as a little boy? Do you have pictures? Videos? Did he always love peanut butter and banana sandwiches fried in a pan? Can I meet the rest of your family? Did he cry when he got that little scar on his elbow as a small boy? Did—*

"Here you are, then." Mrs. Avira pulled a silver chain from her purse. The tiny jade elephant hung from it. "It's his good-luck charm. I know this isn't a competition, but he lent it to me, and I think he should have it back." She held it out.

Misha carefully took it from her. "I'll give it to him right now."

She smiled stiffly. "Well, thank you. I should go find my husband. Have a good show, Mr. Reznikov."

"Please, call me—" He broke off. "Mikhail."

"Then you should call me Jolly." She nodded. "Thank you for delivering my little package. Now I will get going before this young man has palpitations. I'm such a dangerous person, you see?

Can't allow me backstage."

"I don't think you're dangerous!" The guard's face was beet red.

She tsked. "I'm just teasing. So sensitive!" With that she was gone, the jangle of her bracelets echoing as the door thudded shut.

The guard grimaced. "Thanks for your help, man."

"Of course." Misha hurried back with the charm in his hand. His heart raced, and when he spotted Dev with Bailey and some other skaters near the entrance to the rink, nausea flowed through him.

He came to a stop near them and opened his mouth, but no sound came out. He knew he must concentrate on his job, but his breath came shortly, like the wings of a bird were flapping against his ribs. He clutched the necklace, the elephant digging into his palm.

Eyes wide, Dev grabbed hold of Misha's shoulders. "What happened? Are you okay? Are you dizzy?" He turned to Bailey. "Get the medic!"

"*Nyet.*" Misha waved her off. "I...we must speak."

One of the PAs hovering nearby cleared her throat. "Twenty-one minutes to showtime. If you want to use the office there, it's empty."

Misha tried to smile his thanks to her as Dev led him inside. It was a small, barren room with a desk and a few chairs. The gray cement walls were undecorated but for a calendar featuring a picture of a tongue-wagging German shepherd.

"Sit down." Dev guided him to a chair. "I knew you should have rested more."

But Misha shook him off and remained standing. "It is not that." He held out his hand. "Here. From your mother."

Dev blinked. "My...what?" He took the silver chain and caressed the jade elephant. "You saw my mother?"

"She wanted to give it to you, but the guard would not allow it. I told her I would. She insisted you have it back for the show."

"Oh. I…" Dev shook his head. "Thank you? But why are you so upset? Did she say something to you? Whatever it was, I'm sure she didn't mean it. She says a lot of things! It's just the way she is. Her heart's in the right place, I swear."

"It was nothing she said." His throat was bone dry. "It was what I could not say. Vassenka, I cannot go on like this."

Dev's voice was barely a whisper. "What are you saying?"

"To live in fear is to not really live. My father agrees. We spoke earlier. He…" Misha took a deep breath and blew it out. "We agree that the time has come to be truthful. Things are changing in Russia. Perhaps if the people know who I really am, they will look at homosexuals with different eyes. Perhaps I can show my country that we are not the enemy."

"So…what does that mean?"

"I thought I could do this. That I could keep living in secret. But it was different then. I was training in Moscow, and I had no lovers. It was easy to hide. But now there is you, and I don't want to pretend. I want to tell everyone. I want to go to dinner together. Hold your hand on the street and no longer be afraid."

"I do too. God, so much. But we both know the reasons we shouldn't. I don't want things between us to change. I don't want to lose what we have." He swallowed hard. "I'm afraid. Misha, I—"

A sharp knock on the door made them both jump. The PA's voice rang out. "We need all cast members by the tunnel."

They stared at each other in silence.

"Hello? Sorry, but they want you there *now*."

Misha bit his tongue to avoid screaming a curse at the innocent girl. There was nothing left to do but perform their best.

In the main area, Kisa, Bailey, and the other skaters waited.

Kisa gazed at him anxiously and reached up to fiddle with his hair. "You are all right?" she asked quietly.

"Yes," he lied, praying it would become true.

Beside him, Dev fumbled with the clasp on the chain, cursing under his breath as he dropped the charm on the concrete.

"Here, let me help you," Bailey said.

"I've got it!" Dev snapped as he snatched up the necklace. He closed his eyes. "I'm sorry, B. It's not you."

Bailey nodded as she smoothed the skirt of her golden dress, the same that all the women wore for the first number. She glanced at Misha. "Okay. It's cool. We're all cool, right?"

Misha nodded.

"Yeah. It's going to be a great show." Dev tried to smile. He reached around his neck again.

Without thinking, Misha covered Dev's hands with his own. "Let me."

With a shiver, Dev dropped his hands to his sides. Fingers brushing against Dev's neck, Misha did up the clasp and reached around front to tuck the elephant beneath Dev's shirt. Dev gripped his hand almost painfully. Breath frozen, Misha leaned his forehead against Dev's curls.

I can't lose him.

"Okay, everyone! It's almost show time!" Alice clapped. "Remember what I told you..."

As she rattled off her last-minute directions, Misha stood back, and Dev let go of his hand. There may not be medals on the line, but they had a job to do.

Chapter Seventeen

"HAPPY HOLIDAYS, BOSTON! Are you ready for a night of world-class skating?"

As the arena announcer warmed up the crowd, Misha stretched his arms over his head and rolled his neck gingerly. The cast waited in the tunnel created by curtains that exited onto the ice in one of the corners of the rink. They were in line in their places, Kisa at his side and Dev and Bailey in front of them. A PA walked the line.

"We've got a full house tonight, and remember, we're *live*." She walked on, clipboard clutched to her chest.

Bailey snorted. "They do realize that every competition we've ever skated in was live, even if it wasn't televised, right?"

A voice rang out. "Twenty seconds to air!"

"We got this," Bailey declared.

"Sabrina, you're going on three, two, one—go!" A crew member operated a pulley that dramatically swept open the curtains by the ice.

Little Sabrina skated out, and one by one they all followed, Misha and Kisa hand in hand as always. Misha smiled brightly and let his mind go into automatic mode, his body doing the choreography easily. The skaters all wove in and out around each other in an intricate pattern as Mariah Carey's "All I Want for Christmas is You" filled the arena.

Song after song, the show flew by. Misha and Kisa's solo earned a standing ovation from the audience. Despite himself, Misha was able to lose himself in the performance. He smiled and meant it, giving the people the show they deserved.

The arena buzzed, and when Misha, Kisa, Dev, and Bailey took the ice for their group number, the crowd roared. The girls wore white-and-red Santa dresses, with Misha and Dev in black pants and red silk shirts.

As "Up on the Rooftop" played, they performed trick after trick, alternating partners and also gliding down the rink in unison. The grand finale was a lifting sequence, and Misha's back twinged as he pushed Bailey over his head and then turned around to meet Kisa and do the lift again. The audience whistled and applauded, and the four of them took their bows.

Kisa and Bailey skated forward to curtsy while Misha and Dev bowed behind them. As he straightened up, Misha felt a tug on his hand. Heart thumping, he looked at Dev, joy filling him. Dev squeezed his fingers, a smile creasing his beautiful face. Just to hold Dev's hand with everyone watching made a laugh bubble from Misha's chest.

With a grin, Bailey took Dev's other hand, and Kisa skated to Misha's free side. In a line across the ice, they skated back to the tunnel, hands clasped.

Back beyond the curtains, Caroline squealed. "That was so cute! I love it."

One of the producers appeared. "You were supposed to alternate at the end—boy, girl, boy, girl."

"Oops!" Bailey shrugged. "Sorry! Guess we forgot."

Misha and Dev still held hands and stared defiantly until the producer scuttled away, muttering into her headset.

Andrew rolled his eyes. "God, whatever. It's not like you guys made out. What year is this, anyway?"

Surging forward, Bailey planted a kiss on Andrew. "You really are a cool guy, you know that?"

"I—I—" Andrew sputtered, his mouth agape.

Bailey slapped his shoulder and grabbed Dev. "Gotta change for our solo!"

With a squeeze of Misha's hand and a hopeful smile, Dev followed. Andrew stood frozen. Then he lifted his hand to touch his lips.

"It's a Christmas miracle." Grant smirked good-naturedly.

"This American Christmas really is the most wonderful time," Kisa noted. She hugged Misha around his waist and murmured, "That was a beautiful statement, was it not? A good sign. Perhaps there is no need for tears, Misha."

Misha's mind whirled. Was it? Had Dev decided to come out along with him? Was it possible? Or had it only been a fleeting moment? After all, holding hands during a bow was not exactly unheard of. The audience would surely think nothing of it. What did it mean?

"Costume change! Mikhail, you have nine minutes," a PA reminded him.

Again he shut off his brain. The rest of the show was over before he knew it, and Misha found himself milling around in the arena's backstage area. They'd all changed into jeans and sweaters and jackets, but Dev was running behind since he and Bailey had been called away to film a Merry Christmas message for the local station.

Everything will be okay. Be brave. Be brave. Be brave.

"Great show!" said one of the PAs walking by.

Misha nodded and smiled. He took a sip from a bottle of water, and just then, Bailey appeared. She ran past him, and he turned to see her throwing her arms about Mrs. Avira. Misha's pulse rocketed, and his calm evaporated.

"Ma!" Bailey hugged Dev's mother tightly.

Misha searched for Dev, swallowing hard when he was still

nowhere to be found. Kisa appeared, giving him a pat and whispering for him not to worry. Caroline and Grant stood nearby with their parents and shared a meaningful glance.

Bailey took Mrs. Avira's coat and folded it over a nearby chair before hugging Dev's father. "So glad you guys are here."

"You were marvelous! Simply marvelous," Mrs. Avira exclaimed.

The stout man beside her nodded. He was balding and wore glasses and a neatly pressed suit.

"So beautiful out there." She turned to Caroline, Grant, and their parents. "Didn't she look a picture? I'm so proud. I'll never have a daughter-in-law, but I have my Bailey, so I don't need one." She patted Bailey's cheek.

"Ma, you guys remember Caroline and Grant? And their parents?"

Dr. Avira nodded. "How lovely to see you all again. Children, you were wonderful. We hope to see you win Nationals next month."

Mrs. Avira's gaze landed on Misha and Kisa hovering nearby, and her smile froze. At that moment, Dev appeared, and Misha was sure everyone would be able to hear his heart hammering. He clutched his water bottle, the condensation wet on his skin.

"Ma, Dad." Dev hugged them both. "Thanks for coming."

His mother tsked. "As if we would miss such an event, Devassy."

Shoulders tense, Dev turned to Misha and Kisa. "I don't think you guys have all met. Ma, Dad, this is—"

"Of course we know who they are!" Mrs. Avira laughed nervously. "Kisa and Mikhail. Mikhail and I spoke earlier." She nodded politely, as did Dr. Avira.

"No," Dev said. As all eyes swung to him. "I mean, yes, you did, but..." He stepped closer. "Ma, this is Misha."

Frozen, Misha didn't dare blink. Everyone stood motionless,

as if in a tableaux. Dr. Avira tilted his head while his wife stared blankly.

Dev cleared his throat and barreled on. "This is the Misha I'm seeing in California. More than seeing, actually. We're renting a house. We're living together. I'm in love with him. Which I should have told you. And probably in private. Maybe we can go somewhere and talk."

"In love?" Misha blurted.

All activity backstage had halted, and in the silence, Dev laughed uncertainly. "Yeah. I should have told you. Once again probably in private. Definitely in private. But yes, Misha. I'm in love with you."

Misha could barely breathe. The water bottle creaked in his grip.

Dev's gaze skittered away. "Um, I guess this is a shock, and there's no pressure if you don't feel the same. Anyway, I should probably—"

"Of course I feel the same." Misha strode forward, the bottle tumbling to the floor as he threw his arms around Dev. The words flowed like warm honey over his tongue. "I have so much love for you, Vassenka. More than I ever dreamed possible."

"Misha, I've been so wrong." Dev clutched him.

Misha wasn't sure how long they'd been holding each other when they stepped back and faced Dev's parents. In the silence, Mrs. Avira swung her startled gaze to Dev and then back to him, and Misha could hear the blood rushing in his ears. He wondered if he should say something, but any more words were trapped in his throat.

"Ma, Dad, I know this is a shock, and I'm sorry." Dev took Misha's hand. "I should have told you months ago, and I guess I couldn't wait a minute longer."

Dr. Avira spoke quietly. "When did this come about, Devassy?"

"In Annecy. Well, first in Kyoto at the Grand Prix Final, but—"

A chorus of gasps rang out, and Misha realized their audience had grown, with other skaters, families, and production crew all gathered behind him, watching avidly. Mrs. Avira clutched her chest.

"Whoa," Andrew whispered nearby. "Since then? That explains so much."

Bailey addressed Dev's parents. "Okay, so your minds are blown right now, and I totally get it. Been there, done that. But they are really good together. It's totally crazy, but it works. You know I wouldn't give my stamp of approval to just anyone. Misha earned it. That whole cold, imperious thing? He's really not like that. And he makes Dev *so* happy."

As the Aviras took this in silently, Misha thought his heart might explode.

After a deep breath, Dr. Avira held his head a little higher and extended his hand. "Well, then. Good to meet you, Mikhail."

Misha took it gratefully, able to breathe again. "And you, sir. Call me Misha, please." He turned to Dev's mother. "Mrs. Avira, I am very glad to meet you." He held out his hand.

For an endless moment, she stared at it. Then, with a heavy sigh, she batted it away and yanked him into a hug. "I said to call me Jolly."

She was a short woman, and Misha stooped, his back aching, but he didn't care. She smelled of jasmine and cloves, and he held her tightly. When she stepped back, she nodded decisively.

"You will come for Christmas tomorrow." It wasn't a question. She looked to Kisa. "When do you return to Russia?"

Kisa smiled tentatively. "Uh, the twenty-sixth."

"Then you will come tomorrow as well." She turned to her husband. "We must tell Sara not to bring the cardiologist. He'll probably get called into work anyway. Who needs him?" To Dev, she added in a stage whisper, "He isn't very handsome anyway. Not like your Misha." She clucked her tongue. "Even with the bruise. You should protect that face."

Dev kissed her cheek. "I love you, Ma."

"Of course you do. What boy doesn't love his mother? Now, you tell us all about what has been going on in California from the beginning, Devassy." She glanced around at the assembled crowd. "All right, the performance has finished." She shooed, bangles jangling. "Merry Christmas!"

As if a spell was broken, their audience dispersed, the crew going back to work and others saying farewell until only Kisa and Bailey remained with them. They talked quietly off to the side, heads close.

Dev's mother patted her son's cheek. "You are in love, eh? It is about time. I was just saying to Susan Auntie the other day, wasn't I?" She looked at her husband, who nodded.

Misha spoke up. "I truly am in love also." It was so wonderful to say out loud that he felt like laughing at the top of his lungs.

Mrs. Avira nodded vigorously. "Well of course you are in love! Who would not be in love with my son? You would have to be crazy."

"Certifiable," Dr. Avira said. "He is a fine boy."

"He is," Misha agreed.

"I did not know you were also a homosexual, though." Mrs. Avira scrutinized him. "I wouldn't have guessed. What do your parents say? Have they met Devassy? Tell us about them," Mrs. Avira commanded.

"Not yet. My family will visit this spring." Misha glanced at Dev. "Perhaps you could visit as well?"

Dev nodded. "That would be great. Dad, can you take some time off?"

"Of course he can! When did your father last take a vacation? So long ago I can barely remember. Let the other surgeons do some work for a change."

And just like that, they made plans for the future, with talk of Disneyland and the Santa Monica pier, and Misha smiled so much his face hurt.

BY THE TIME he and Dev left for the hotel after seeing the Aviras off, Misha was pleasantly worn out, the adrenaline high after performing fading. Bailey and Kisa climbed into the transport van outside, but Misha enjoyed breathing in the frosty air. "Can we walk?" he asked Dev.

"Sure. It's not too far."

A fresh layer of snow blanketed the streets, and only a few cars went by. Fat flakes of snow drifted down, peppering Dev's black hair. The wind was calm, and as they strolled along, gloved hands clasped, Misha breathed in the night air deeply. The city was aglow with Christmas colors—lights and wreaths and decorations glittering amid the snow.

"I can't believe I was so afraid to tell my parents. I should have given them more credit. But I'm sorry it was so public. I was planning on telling them in private, but as soon as I saw them standing there with you, I couldn't keep it in another second."

"I do not mind. It was…" Misha tried to find the right words. "It felt good to be declared. Do you know what I mean?"

Dev kissed him lightly. "I know exactly what you mean."

In the stillness as they walked, voices raised in song murmured, growing stronger as Dev and Misha neared a church.

"*It came upon the midnight clear, that glorious song of old.*"

Dev checked his watch. "It's almost Christmas. I know you don't celebrate it until January, though."

"I will mark it twice. There is much to celebrate, yes?"

Dev grinned. "Da."

As they reached the church, the choir echoed into the night from within. "*The world in solemn stillness lay, to hear the angels sing.*"

"What will tomorrow be like?" Misha asked.

"Chaos. A lot of food and a lot of people. I may be an only child, but I have a ton of cousins. Everyone usually comes over by around three. We don't sit at the table—not enough room. So Ma and my aunties put all the food out there, and it's a buffet, and you find a place to sit wherever—living room, kitchen, den. It'll be mostly Indian food, but turkey and stuffing as well. Sara Auntie makes the best cranberry sauce from scratch."

"Do you think they'll like me?" His gut twisted foolishly, as if he was a mere boy.

"Of course. Just be yourself." Dev smiled as they crossed the street, the snow falling more thickly now. "They'll love you."

"It shall be a shock to them, though. That we are together."

Dev smirked. "It'll be a shock to them tonight when they hear all about it from my mother. Trust me, by tomorrow, the whole family will know. Probably the entire south Indian population in Boston too. Make that the eastern seaboard."

Misha was chuckling when he skidded on the sidewalk, sneakers slipping on an icy patch hidden by the fresh snow. Clutching at Dev, he windmilled his free arm, but they tumbled to the ground, landing on their rear ends in an ungainly heap.

"*Ow.* Thanks for bringing me down with you." Dev elbowed him playfully. "We're getting too old for this. How many years have we spent on ice? Can't even stay on our feet now. This is humiliating."

The snow was a couple of inches thick now, covering the lights strung around the trees arching overhead. The sidewalk was empty except for them, the streets quiet in the lull before midnight mass concluded. "Since we are down here..." Misha extended himself into the pristine snow covering the church lawn.

With arms and legs out, he flapped them up and down. "*Snezhnyy* angel."

Brushing off his jeans uselessly, Dev got to his feet and then launched himself farther over on the lawn. He waved his limbs, their gloves touching on each pass. "I haven't done this since I was a kid. We're going to be soaked."

"We'll have to take a long, hot bath together."

"Sounds terrible."

"Yes. A very bad Christmas."

"The worst."

Misha stared at Dev flapping beside him in the snow. *We love each other.* He could hardly believe it was real, but nothing had ever felt so true.

As the clock struck twelve, they made angels and listened to the choir's new song.

"*All is calm, all is bright...*"

Epilogue

IT WAS DARK by the time Misha turned toward the ocean. He'd splurged on a fancy entertainment system in his Honda, and at least it made being stuck in LA traffic more bearable. He'd agreed to visit the reopening training center up at Lake Arrowhead as a favor for a friend of Dev's boss, but the slow drive back into the city had him gripping the steering wheel and cursing under his breath. It was New Year's Eve, yet rush hour was unchanged.

"This is why I prefer to stay on the beach," he muttered to himself.

It had been pleasant to work with the young pair team and give them advice. He had no interest in coaching, but it was a birthday surprise for the girl, who'd shrieked and gone very red in the face when he'd skated onto the ice without warning. They'd taken many pictures, and she'd cried a little and asked him to autograph just about everything in her backpack. As a special treat, he had worked with her on a simple lasso lift and whirled her high around the ice faster than her partner could dream of going at his level.

Misha smiled to himself. It had been a good day, even though he'd missed writing. He had story ideas turning over and over in his mind, and at least in the creeping traffic he'd been able to dictate a few into his new phone.

Still, by the time he parked in the driveway, he was tired and ready for a cold beer and quiet night. Dev was working until seven o'clock, and sure enough, the house was dark. Misha had wanted to have a proper celebration, but Dev hadn't seemed very interested. Still, Misha would make an Olivier salad at least.

As Misha walked to the green-painted front door, he frowned at the shut curtains. He was sure he'd left them open. He and Dev rarely closed any of the drapes, preferring to let the sunlight stream in.

Misha turned his key and opened the door. There was only silence. *Not as though a thief would go to the trouble of closing the drapes anyway.* But as he blinked, he realized there was a strange, soft glow coming from the rear of the house. He called out, "Dev? You are here?"

No answer. Misha had dropped off Zoloto with the neighbor before leaving for Lake Arrowhead, so no doggie rushed to greet him. A strange feeling prickled his spine. *Something is not right.* Shutting the door behind him, Misha tiptoed around the corner to the open living room, where they had their couch and television with a view of the beach and ocean beyond. "*Bozhe moi!*"

The large pine tree stood in the corner by the sliding doors to the patio, casting its colored light across the light wood and high to the soaring ceiling—red, pink, green, blue, and yellow. Sparkling ornaments hung from it, and a golden glass spire shone from the top. Beside it was Dev, dressed in a blue velvet cloak and long hat, both trimmed with white fur and adorned with glittering snowflakes.

"Sorry, Dev's not here. I'm Father Frost. Happy New Year."

Delight surged through Misha as he laughed. "I cannot believe it, Vassenka. You have done this for me?"

"Of course." Dev motioned to the tree. "Kisa brought some of the ornaments. The hanging nesting dolls are amazing." He spread his arms wide, revealing that he was naked beneath the thick cloak. "And of course she brought me the outfit. You like?"

Misha closed the distance between them and hauled Dev into his arms. "Very much." He chuckled to himself. "Father Frost has never been so sexy. And I see this is why Kisa brought such large suitcases. You planned this before she arrived?"

Dev straightened the floppy end of his hat. "Yep. I e-mailed and asked about what you like to do for the holidays. I know it's hard that you're away from home." He waved a hand over himself with a shrug. "This is kind of silly, but I thought you might like it."

Misha found he could not stop grinning. "It is all I could dream of. This is my home. There is no better place for me."

With a beaming smile, Dev kissed him. "I never thought it could be like this. Not much more than a year ago, you were practically a stranger." His fingers were soft on Misha's face. "God, I used to hate you so much, and now you're everything."

Misha leaned their foreheads together. "We are the team now. Maybe we do not skate together, but you are my partner."

"Always."

They held each other, and Misha buried his face in the soft material of Dev's cloak. When they kissed, it was sweet and gentle at first, and Misha thought he could be forever happy like that, kissing Dev in the rainbow glow of the tree. But soon his blood roared, and he tugged at his clothing until they were both naked on top of the cloak, spread wide on the wooden floor. They loved each other with mouths and hands, bodies entwined, giving pleasure until they were spent and tangled.

Dev brushed back Misha's sweat-damp hair from his forehead. "So if I'm Father Frost, do I grant your New Year's wish? The way we'd ask Santa Claus for something we really want?"

Misha pressed a kiss to Dev's neck, where his pulse still fluttered. "I have used my wish. What will yours be?"

Zoloto's excited barking from the beach jolted them both. With a groan, Dev pushed himself up and shrugged on the cloak. "Carol said she'd drop her back around nine." He waved through the glass.

Misha sat up and waved as well to their neighbor, too sated

and warm to care about his nakedness. Zoloto bounded across the wooden deck, and Carol's laughter echoed on the waves as Dev opened the sliding door.

"Thanks, Carol! We owe you!" Dev called.

She waved, still laughing as she headed home.

Zoloto exploded through the door, skidding on the floor as she raced to Misha and then back to Dev, tongue hanging out as she spun around. Dev scooped her up and kissed her head.

"How's our girl? Are you going to help me get dinner ready? Or are you going to knock ornaments off the tree and slobber everywhere?"

Zoloto barked and licked his face.

"I think she says the second option is best." Misha laughed. "Here, I will take her. Are you making traditional Russian New Year's dinner? Or your famous frozen meatballs?"

With a flourish, Dev scooped up the velvet hat and set it on his head. "Father Frost is insulted you would even ask." He pivoted on his heel and marched toward the kitchen. At the door, he turned. "And yes, meatballs. Also a salad Kisa gave me a recipe for. And some pizza pockets and a key lime cheesecake. It's a Russian/American mash-up."

Misha grinned. "Sounds perfect."

Just before midnight, they were snuggled on the couch in their pajamas with the blue velvet cloak as a blanket, Zoloto tucked between them. Misha nudged Dev with his shoulder. "You never gave me your New Year's wish."

The countdown from Times Square began on TV. Of course it had been recorded earlier on the East Coast, but Misha still felt the tingle of anticipation. *"Ten, nine, eight—"*

Dev breathed deeply and took Misha's hand. "Just...this."

"Three, two, one—Happy New Year!"

As Zoloto howled, they kissed, and the future began.

THE END

Afterword

Thank you so much for reading and I hope you enjoyed it. I'd be grateful if you could take a few minutes to leave a review on Goodreads (or wherever you'd like!). Just a couple of sentences can really help other readers discover this book. Thank you!

Join the free gay romance newsletter!

My (mostly) monthly newsletter will keep you up to date on my latest releases and news from the world of LGBTQ romance. You'll also get access to exclusive giveaways, free reads, and much more. Join the mailing list today and you're automatically entered into my monthly giveaway.

Here's where you can find me online:
Website
www.keiraandrews.com
Facebook
facebook.com/keira.andrews.author
Facebook Reader Group
bit.ly/2gpTQpc
Instagram
instagram.com/keiraandrewsauthor
Goodreads
bit.ly/2k7kMj0
Amazon Author Page
amzn.to/2jWUfCL
Twitter
twitter.com/keiraandrews
BookBub
bookbub.com/authors/keira-andrews

Read more sports romance from Keira Andrews!

The Next Competitor

If he risks his heart, can he keep his head in the game?

To win gold, figure skater Alex Grady must train harder than the competition morning, noon, and night. He's obsessed with mastering another quadruple jump, and due to the lack of filter between his mouth and brain, doesn't have a lot of friends. As for a boyfriend, forget it. So what if he's still a virgin at twenty? The Olympics are only every four years—everything else can wait. Relationships are messy and complicated anyway, and he has zero room in his life for romance.

So it's ridiculous when Alex finds himself checking out his boring new training mate Matt Savelli. Calm, collected "Captain Cardboard" is a nice guy, but even if Alex had time to date, Matt's so not his type. Yet beneath Matt's wholesome surface, there's a dirty, sexy man who awakens a desire Alex has never experienced and can't deny...

This gay romance from Keira Andrews features opposites attracting, new adult angst, sexual discovery, and of course a happy ending.

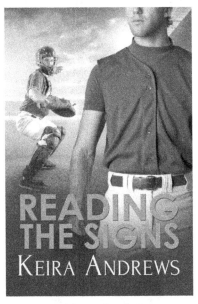

Reading the Signs

This hot-headed rookie needs discipline—on and off the field.

Pitcher Nico Agresta is desperate to live up to his family's baseball legacy. Since he was a teenager crushing on his big brother's teammate, he's known he can't act on his desires. His father's made it clear there should be no queers on the field, but if Nico can win Rookie of the Year like his dad and brother did, maybe he can prove he's worthy after all.

At 34, veteran catcher Jake Fitzgerald just wants to finish out his contract and retire. His team doesn't have a prayer of making the playoffs, but who needs the stress? Jake lost his passion for the game—and life—after driving away the man he loved, and he swore he'd never risk his heart again.

Then he's traded to a team that wants a vet behind the plate to tame their new star pitcher. Jake is shocked to find the gangly kid he once knew has grown into a gorgeous young man. But tightly wound Nico's having trouble controlling his temper in his quest for perfection, and Jake needs to teach him patience and restraint on the mound.

When their push and pull explodes into the bedroom, Nico and Jake will both learn how much they'll risk for love.

This gay sports romance from Keira Andrews features men who have been repressing their feelings far too long, light BDSM, an age difference, sweaty locker rooms, and of course a happy ending.

About the Author

After writing for years yet never really finding the right inspiration, Keira discovered her voice in gay romance, which has become a passion. She writes contemporary, historical, paranormal, and fantasy fiction, and—although she loves delicious angst along the way—Keira firmly believes in happy endings. For as Oscar Wilde once said, "The good ended happily, and the bad unhappily. That is what fiction means."

Find out more about Keira's books and sign up for her (mostly) monthly gay romance e-newsletter:

keiraandrews.com

CPSIA information can be obtained
at www.ICGtesting.com
Printed in the USA
FSHW011426190420
69353FS

9 781988 260525